roman

New York Times and USA Today Bestselling Author

HEIDI MCLAUGHLIN
AND AMY BRIGGS

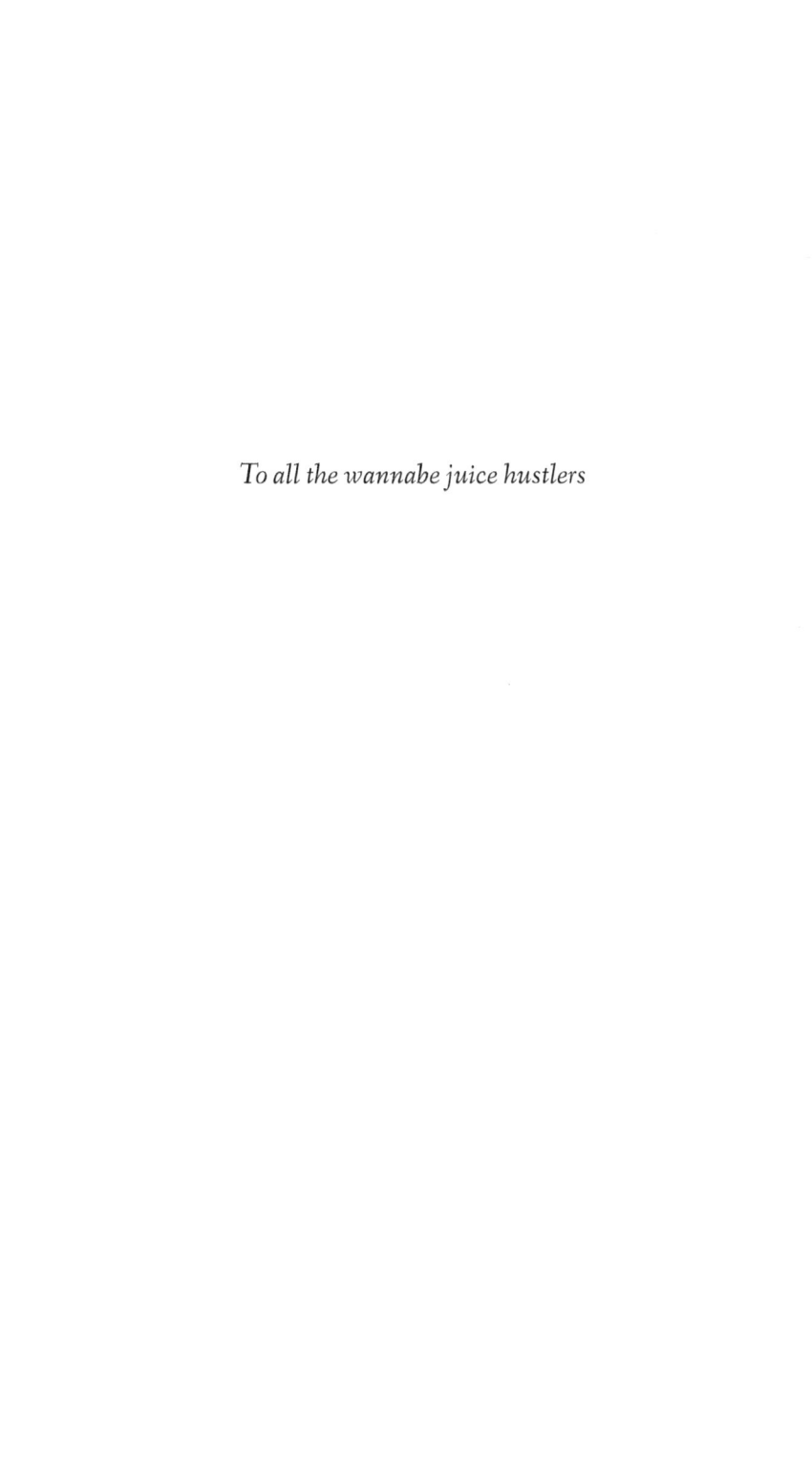

To all the wannabe juice hustlers

ROMAN
THE CLUTCH SERIES #1
HEIDI MCLAUGHLIN
AMY BRIGGS
© 2018

COVER DESIGN: Letitia Hasser ~ RBA Designs.
EDITING: Kellie Montgomery

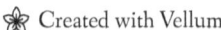

1

ROMAN

*L*ights flash, like an eternal disco, lighting up the night sky. Nobody visiting keeps time in Las Vegas, the true city that never sleeps. Faces race by slowly, my heightened vision enabling me to make out every feature, from a crooked nose to fake eyelashes. Tourists from all over the world flock to the desert. Some to vacation in the sun, some hoping for their big break, others desperate for a fresh start. Everyone needs a change of pace or something different every now and again, even myself.

The humidity from the building, the people, and the general metropolis Las Vegas has become, traps the heat on the Strip. I prefer the area just outside of the city, where the desert is cooler, where the sun retreats behind the mountains in the distance, and the crisp air is free of the city pollution. Each night, as the sun begins to tuck itself into bed, the pink reflection left on the mountainside is meditative. I try to catch the sunset every evening, as it has brought a calm and peaceful appreciation for my surroundings. When you've lived as long as I have, finding moments of serenity are a rare gift.

My impatience grows as I continue to wait for Melody with whom I had an appointment twenty minutes ago. Humans are always late and full of selfish excuses for it. When she arrives, her face is flushed, and her chest is heaving slightly as she catches her breath.

"Roman. I am so sorry I'm late."

"I was beginning to wonder if you changed your mind about working with me." She hasn't, I can tell by the racing of her heart. She's nervous, not because of what I am, but out of the fear that I'll dismiss her. She knows a big commission when she sees one. To me from the moment we met was evident, and if I didn't have more specific standards in consorts, I might have taken her up on her advances, as she was easy prey.

"You know you're my favorite client." Her head tilts to the left, showing me her jugular. My tongue darts out, passing over my razor-sharp teeth. Melody doesn't wear a cross, meaning she'd be perfectly comfortable if I were to compel her, but I refrain. Not because I'm in public, but more so because I'm trying to keep business away from pleasure. However, allowing Melody to think she has a chance is no exception. Pleasure always seems to win out in the end.

Over the years, the ability to pick up and play off of human weaknesses has become second nature. "Yes, well, then let's get down to business, shall we?" The casino property that I want to purchase has just gone on the market. The current owners had no idea what they were getting into when they bought it. Renovations and upkeep to accommodate millions of people running through the doors of casinos require significant work and operational management. It's not as simple as putting your name on the deed and collecting the cash that rolls in.

"Of course. Again, I'm so sorry I'm late." She reaches

into her bag and pulls out a large blue folder with her company's logo on the front, and hands it to me. "Here is the prospectus for the property. A full view of everything top to bottom. Would you like to look at them over a drink?" She smiles, with a hopeful look in her eyes.

"I believe you already know I don't drink." I smirk at her, acknowledging her proposition. I had to give her an A for effort. She didn't lay it on too thick but made her intentions known nonetheless.

"That's right, I almost forgot." She grins, shrugging her shoulders.

"Let's walk around the place again so that I can be sure I know what I need to before filing the formal papers." I tuck the folder under my arm, not reviewing it. I've already seen the blueprints of the property; in fact, I have them memorized. I know exactly what I'm getting into. However, achieving a certain level of comfort with the people I have to do business with is of the utmost importance. The only questions I have remaining are ensuring I file the necessary paperwork with the municipality and the gaming commission.

We walk silently around the exterior of the building before going inside to talk. Melody picks at the skin on her thumb nervously, waiting for me to speak once we sit down at a bar table inside the casino.

"Are you nervous around me, Melody?" I ask sardonically.

Dropping her hands to her lap, she shakes her head. "No, Roman. Not at all. I mean I've never done business with a vampire before, but it's no big deal. Just like doing business with anyone else. I think you are all great." She rambles.

"You can relax Melody. You do know that we don't go

around biting people whenever we want. That is unless we're invited of course," I reply smoothly. I'm flirting back, and while I have no interest in feeding off her, or fucking her for that matter, it's a behavior that is instinctive. Vampires by nature are virile. It's a glorious affliction to be attractive to the opposite sex and to have the ability to pick and choose, which wasn't always the case. For many years we hid, unable to walk among the humans as we do now. They hunted us, killing off the population because of who we are.

"Oh, I know." She grins, shifting in her seat. "My friend says you only bite people who want to be bitten."

"Your friend is correct." My eyes shift, watching her turn her engagement ring around her finger until I force myself to focus on the issue at hand, buying the casino. "So, Melody, I'm in. I want you to broker this deal. I'd like to expedite this process though as quickly as possible. I have plans to renovate immediately, and subsequently, I have plans to construct an additional unrelated building with the net gains from this property. So, the contract needs to include not only this casino but the empty lot that we discussed outside of downtown as well. Can you handle this?"

"Of course I can. Have you filed the necessary permits with the gaming commission or the township?"

"Yes and no. My permits to renovate are filed; however, I'm unclear exactly what needs to be done with the gaming commission. Doesn't the property come with the license?" I've tried looking into this, but the information provided on the commission's website is archaic at best, and that says a lot, coming from a five hundred-year-old vampire.

"I was afraid of that." She purses her lips thoughtfully as if she has more to add.

"What is it?" I demand.

"You have to file for your own gaming license. There's a set number available, and yours will be the one that's given up by the current owners. But, there's a bit of a snag we haven't discussed yet." The ring twisting has stopped, and she looks at me with pure fear in her eyes. Not responding, I raise my eyebrows at her, and gently spin my hand for her to continue.

"Well, the head of the gaming commission... he's a difficult man. And, as it turns out, he doesn't like to do business with vampires. As in, he won't give you a license. But, not to worry. Now, what I suggest you do, is find yourself a human who you can trust, and have them file the paperwork to get the license," she explains hesitantly.

"So, you're saying I can't actually own my own casino? I have to get a business partner, which I do not want, by the way, to act as my surrogate so that I can get this piece of paper?"

"Unless you can come up with a way to warm him up to vampires, then yes. That is exactly what I'm saying. I realize you weren't looking for a partnership, but in this town, the gaming commissioner is the head honcho. They... well he, controls everything. And Mr. Weston is quite known for his anti-vampire stance."

"Mr. Weston," I repeat quietly. Going straight to the sore spot on a sensitive subject such as this seems irresponsible. It took hundreds of years for vampires to be able to walk about freely, openly as vampires, and for the holdouts to the cause, it was never a good idea to become confrontational. This is going to take some degree of finesse.

"Yes, Mr. James Weston. He is who you're going to need approval from. All gaming licenses require his signature. Once you have that, we can move forward with the deal. But, until then, I can keep it pending under contract, so another buyer doesn't swoop in."

I lean forward, placing my palms on top of Melody's hands. As she meets my gaze, I whisper, "You will make sure that no one else gets this property, right Melody?"

Under my compulsion, her eyes glaze over as she nods slowly. "I will make sure no one else gets this property."

"Thank you, Melody."

"Of course, Roman," she mutters quietly, still under my artificial rapture.

"I will be in touch." I stand up, grasping the folder with the blueprints and plans in it, and shove it back under my arm. I repeat the name of the obstacle in my way over and over as I make my way toward the exit. I need to find a way to turn this Mr. Weston into an ally, instead of a vampire fearing foe. As I walk out of the casino, the various voices around me are a stark reminder that humans are vain. Each one has a price, a weakness of some kind, a social ladder they need to climb, and when someone with my power, resources, and income comes along with a proposition, they buckle at the knees, begging to do business with me. It won't take much for me to figure out how feeble Mr. Weston is. If anything, I'm more determined now than ever to buy this property. As far as I'm concerned, Mr. Weston has no idea what he's in for.

2

FIONA

"*H*e's so hot," my friend Lana says as the waiter walks by. Normally, behind my darkened sunglasses, I can stare freely, but the man in the all-too-tight white shorts with his matching polo carries the mark of a vampire. If I didn't notice the symbol on his hand, the pale legs are a dead giveaway. No pun intended.

"He's a vampire," Leslie whispers as if she thinks he or the many people around us cannot hear her. "An abomination. My daddy says..."

This is where I tune her out. Leslie and her fake Southern accent, along with Lana, have been my best friends since middle school. We're as close as sisters, but frenemies all the same. High society rich girls, living off our daddy's trust funds, doing nothing but lounging by the pool during the day, and partying all night. At least, that is how my father's new wife described us to her tea drinking, silver dyed haired women's group. For the life of me, I will never understand why women choose to dye their hair gray. It seems cool but makes me wonder if they're going through some early mid-life crisis. Surely, their boyfriends and husbands don't appreciate it.

"You know, Leslie, don't knock it until you try it." I turn my head in time to see Lana pulling down her sunglasses and winking at Leslie, whose mouth drops open in complete horror.

"Are you saying you've been with a vamp?" I ask, swinging my legs around the side of the chaise lounge so I can face Lana.

"Repeatedly."

Leslie shrieks. "You lost your flower to a dead person? Wait, are they considered people?"

I roll my eyes and glance over my shoulder to see where the vampire server is; not that he can't hear us, but from the looks of it, he looks like he's ignoring us. Either that or he's plotting our demise later. "Leslie, why do you insist on calling your virginity a flower? And yes, they're people." I think. Honestly, I don't know much about the vampires, other than they've walked the earth for a couple hundred years, but it's been the last hundred or so where our government has controlled them, put sanctions on the way they live their lives. They have rules to follow, just like humans.

"My mama--"

"La la la, time to grow up, Leslie. Seriously, I popped my cherry freshman year in high school. Surely, you remember me telling the both of you." Lana shakes her head, probably out of disbelief or aggravation. Lord knows Leslie tries my patience on a daily basis with her holier-than-thou act. Honestly, I'm surprised she's showing as much skin as she is right now because it's against her religion. "Anyway, I met Marc at the gym. He's a personal trainer, and well let me just say, he trained me well in the locker room."

"Lana..."

"...You're going to go to hell," Leslie blurts out before I can finish what I was going to say. Although, I'm somewhat thankful for her outburst because the truth is, I haven't the slightest idea of what I should say to my friend. To each their own, of course, but I'm not sure I could do it. Be with someone who for the most part is dead and yet insanely hot. That's the one thing vamps have going for them; they're gorgeous, but it's all a ruse. They're meant to be undeniably attractive, so we forget our wits and succumb to their ways. For as long as I can remember, I've always worn a cross. It doesn't necessarily protect me from being compelled, but those who carry the mark are supposed to respect my wishes not to be.

"She's not going to hell, Leslie. Lana is free to make her own choices."

"But to bed a dead man, it's against nature."

"I don't understand what the big deal is, Leslie. They walk, talk, and groom themselves like we do. They work, pay taxes and are contributing members of society. So what if their heart doesn't beat; everything else works." Lana shrugs as if having a non-functioning vital organ is the same as last season's Louis Vuitton bag, which I can easily say I'd never get caught dead with.

"Did he bite you?" I ask, titling my head to the right and then the left to see if I can spot any teeth marks. There are ample women around town who have bite marks on their necks. They show them visibly, almost as if they wear them with pride.

Lana fans herself, although the motion of her hand will do nothing to curb the boiling heat. Her smile is wide as she angles her head to the side. Her finger trails down her neck and her eyes close, almost as if she remembers the moment his fangs punctured her skin. She points to a spot, but it's faint, and the only way I can see is if I stand and lean over Leslie, who is refusing to look. "I don't see anything."

"I have cover-up on."

"Why?" I sit back down, but can't seem to tear my eyes away from her neck. "If you're so proud of being with him, surely you want people to know."

"Because she knows it's wrong." Leslie picks up the magazine and violently turns the pages. Her breathing is picking up; her chest is heaving more rapidly than normal. I've known her long enough to know she's about to explode into some sort of diva-style hissy fit, unloading her wrath of righteousness on all of us. I'm not sure if I agree or disagree with her, as I've never been in the position to make a choice when it comes to socializing with the undead. For all my life, my father has warned me against having an association with them, and honestly, Lana is the first of my friends to admit she's been with a vampire. I'd be lying if I said I wasn't interested in knowing more, but knowledge and experience are two different things.

"You only think it's wrong because you've never tried it, Leslie." Lana swings her legs to the side of the chaise and reaches toward Leslie's leg. She pulls away, angling herself toward me. I fear Lana's choice of bedmates will inevitably ruin our friendship. "My parents," Lana pauses and looks up to the sky. I do the same, wondering what's caught her attention. There's nothing I see, not a plane, a cloud or even a bird flying by, and it's not like she's looking toward heaven since both her parents are still alive. "They asked that I keep my love life private."

"Because it's wrong," Leslie spits.

"They know?" I ask. "I mean, of course, they know if they asked you, but you know..." Lana trails off. She doesn't need to finish her sentence because I do know. The people our families associate with, they're against vampires having any sort of freedom. I'm not sure where I stand, mostly because I've never had any interaction with them.

"Your parents are probably disgusted by what you've done; how you allowed your body to be violated by a dead thing."

"Leslie--"

"Can we talk about something else?" I interrupt Lana before she goes off on Leslie, wanting to steer my two best friends to something different. Having my friends fight over this is the last thing I want. Lana should've known better than to say anything. We both know where Leslie stands on this issue.

Leslie sets her magazine down and spins in my direction, her knees crashing into mine. Her hands are clasped, but the look on her face tells me she's about to flip her bitch switch off and go back to being the sweet and loving friend she is. "Like the party, you're having?" Her eyes light up, and her frown turns into a glowing smile. Party. It's Leslie's favorite word. Mine too, to be honest.

"Or Louis Vuitton's new line?" I hedge. In a matter of hours the store will be filled with everything I want, but don't need.

"Or the fact that Britney has ended her residency here and we're left with JLo?" Lana asks. I glance at her, and she shrugs. "What? I like Britney."

"But not Lopez?" I ask. I'm rather shocked, considering Lopez has been married to her vampire for years now and was one of the more famous people to announce a union with one.

She shakes her head. "She's good, but...eh."

Leslie rolls her eyes, and I can already tell there's going

to be a strain on our friendship. It'll take days, maybe weeks, but Leslie will start asking me to do things with only her, leaving me to choose between my friends. I hate the idea. "Your party," she says, reaching for my hands. "It has to be off the hook, amazing, with only the best of the best in attendance."

"Aren't all my parties like this?" Hosting parties is what I'm good at. It's how I earn a living, so to speak. I do this for my father; entertain investors when they come to town so they'll want to do business here. Not that there's much space for expansion on the Strip, but my dad is looking to increase the area by extending the Strip, which is something the locals aren't happy with. My father and I don't always see eye to eye, but he's willing to keep my bank account full as long as I'm doing my part and making sure the right businesses are coming to town. This isn't how I saw using my business degree, but I have to admit the perks are nice. My penthouse is paid for, I have a car service and a black American Express that yes, my daddy covers, but it's for his cause, not mine. I'm at a stage in my life where I'm not sure I know what I want to do so until then, I'll happily live off my daddy's money, especially if it means my current step-mommy doesn't get it all.

"Some are stuffy, boring," Lana adds. "You should have a midnight soirée. Picture this: white lights everywhere setting a romantic mood with soft music playing in the background."

"So your freak friends can come?" Leslie's words have a lot of bite, no pun intended.

"Sounds like all my parties," I point out, hoping to get back on topic before Leslie and Lana go at it.

"For your uneducated mind, vampires walk among us,

Leslie. They don't only come out at night or sleep in coffins."

Leslie looks at me; she smiles and starts to gather her stuff. "I can't sit here anymore." She stands and without another word, walks back toward the hotel.

"What's her problem?" Lana asks as she slides over to the now vacated chair. "She thinks she's better than us."

"Everyone has their own beliefs."

"And what are yours?"

I look over at Lana, taking her all in. She's tall, slender and her hair always makes the perfect messy bun. Every time I see her with one, I'm jealous because mine is either flat, my extensions show or I have so much product in my hair it hurts to touch. "I don't know," I tell her honestly. "You're the first person I know who has admitted to being with one and liking it. I've heard horror stories though."

"Loving," she corrects me. "Fiona, I had never been treated so amazingly by a man until that moment. And those stories you hear, it's because the media wants to scare you. It's all propaganda by the government to strike fear in the humans."

"But he bit you."

"Only after he asked." Her hand comes up to her neck, and she smiles. "When I saw him at the gym, I could tell there was a spark. He didn't have to compel me either; I went willingly. And it wasn't like we met and bam. We talked, flirted, laughed. I suggested it because I wanted him, whether he's human or not."

I want to be happy for my friend, and maybe I am. I turn back toward the pool and survey the crowd. The vampire waiter is across the way, chatting up some women. He leans down, almost as if he's going to whisper something, only he cradles her head in his hand. It doesn't take a genius to figure out what he's doing. He's biting her, out in public for all of us to see. I feel like I should say something, but my voice will be ignored. Either he's compelled her or she's invited him in, which is none of my business, and yet I find myself staring, watching. My hand goes to my neck and Lana chuckles beside me.

"It's the most amazing feeling in the world," she says. "Let me know when you want to try it. I can hook you up."

Tearing my eyes away from the scene across from me, I gather my belongings and stand. "Louis is about to open up, let's go." I don't wait for Lana to follow behind because I know she will, she always does.

3

ROMAN

I spent the better half of two days researching everything I could find about James Weston, from scouring the Internet to following him around silently, observing. Much like hunting prey, I stalked him. He has an ex-wife, living off his fortune via a sizable alimony settlement in California, and new, younger wife living with him here in Las Vegas with strangely colored hair. Being as old as I am, there are some fashion trends I cannot get behind, and young women dyeing their hair an odd silver gray prematurely is one of them. The most fruitful bit of my research was finding out Weston has a daughter. A beautiful, socialite daughter, who looks to be my ticket to getting what I want.

Though I found her incredibly attractive when I came across her pictures, she appears as empty as most humans, if not more. She had managed to get herself a business degree in college; however, it seems she is doing nothing more than socializing, shopping and spending her father's money, which leads me to believe she is definitely daddy's little girl. Perfect for me. Girls who dote on their fathers are generally easily swayed by my inherent charm, and I plan to make sure she is no different. Win the favor or even the lust of the daughter— get my casino. The perfect plan.

With my plan in place, I set out to run into her in a seemingly accidental manner. It continues to baffle me how easily you can find out about people on the Internet, which informed me that she hung out at a swanky pool club many afternoons, and fortunately for me, I have a friend who works there as a waiter. As luck would have it, she's exactly where her social media account said she was: with friends, and much to my delight they're talking about sleeping with vampires.

Grinning, I continue to listen from afar, blocking out the other mindless chatter surrounding me. This group of women is the only thing interesting me right now, and I really want to know what they have planned for the rest of their afternoon.

The fact she has no real opinion on vampires bodes well in my favor. I can use this to my advantage, striking up a conversation and putting her at ease before I go in for the kill, so to speak. It's her initial reaction to her friend spilling the little tidbit about sleeping with a vampire that has me leaning forward even though it's unnecessary for me to do so. I observe the way her body reacts to her friend's tale of a romp in a locker room with a vampire. I can feel her intrigue, but also her heart rate increases as though she's nervous in some way, which piques my interest. She's never been with a vampire, but she's thought about it. I can feel a smirk form, knowing that I'm going to charm her. I think it will be rather enjoyable.

At first glance, it may seem callous or cold to target her, but it's not like she's some kind of saint. I am positioning myself to run into her shopping for Louis Vuitton for

Christ's sake, which sounds like she has plenty of, simply because they're releasing new items today. If that isn't the vainest and superfluous way to spend a Thursday afternoon, I don't know what is. As I wait to stalk them shopping, I wonder what is taking them so long to get ready.

It's easy to go unnoticed in Las Vegas, getting lost in the crowds, which is why it's one of my favorite cities that I've lived in over the years. With new faces every day, I blend in easily, walking among the humans, with the exception of my mark. Each of us is branded with the Mark of the Fates, from the day we are born again as vampires. Much of the lore in the movies and in the media is complete bullshit. The reality is, we vampires have our own hierarchy and societal expectations to abide by, far outside of the rules we agree to follow amongst the humans. We all used to be human at one point, this much is true. But I can follow the girls in broad daylight; I won't burst into flames or sparkle for that matter, and with the exception of my very pale skin, and my Mark of the Fates, I can go undetected as a human if I choose to, which generally I do.

I'm a businessman by nature, and I've never been a controversial vampire. When I first turned, I had a bit of fun running around before there were any understandings between vampires and humans, but I've never fed on anyone without their permission. I never wanted to be a poster child or role model of any kind for vampires either. I've always enjoyed starting new businesses, successful companies or ventures that I build myself. The satisfaction of creating something that lives on has lit a fire in me for as long as I can remember. Many, in fact, most, vampires are wealthy because over time we invest, and we live to see the fruits of our labor. This casino is important to me. More than any of the other enterprises I've taken on.

I see her through the window of the store; her shiny blonde hair is held out of her face with designer sunglasses perched on her head, thankful her vampire-hating friend known as Leslie decided not to join her. Fiona's tongue darts out, wetting her plump pink lips, toying with the cross dangling from her neck. The rule is if someone wears a cross, they're off limits from our compulsion, which means I'm going to have to spend time getting to know her. Leaving us no choice but to meet and talk.

As I continue to observe her fondling the new purses with her friend, Lana, I formulate how I'll do it. Approaching her now isn't going to work. I need a new plan, a moment where Fiona Weston happens to me and not the other way around.

"So Fiona, what's this party for exactly?" I turn sharply when I hear this question. I heard mention of a party earlier but brushed it off as another socialite function meant to bore me until now. This is where I could spend time with her. I need to get an invitation to this party.

I continue to listen, hoping to find out more when the friend called Lana brings up the very event. "It's a gathering of investors. People with too much money and time on their hands who want to throw millions at the casinos. There's a few of them that are for sale you know, so people are always looking for money."

"Wait, there are casinos for sale?" she asks, seeming surprised. All I can think is how ill-informed this lot is.

"Of course there are. There always are. It's not like the casinos hammer a sign out in front of them though, geez. We're talking about millions of dollars here. There's got to be wheeling and dealing with anything in Vegas." Fiona laughs. She seems to understand how things work, but it's likely because she's overheard it from her father.

"Well then, how do people know anything is for sale?"

"Because it's not for sale to just anyone. This party is for those people to get to know each other and talk about what's available and that sort of thing. It's like a mixer for investors and casinos, in this case, looking for investors. Essentially, it's a private gathering for all of these people to spend money and find new people to make money with. And, they all know my dad of course." It seems perhaps she knows a bit more about business than I initially gave her credit for.

I continue to listen as the girls discuss the party, which I'm now certain is where I'll make inroads with this pretty little thing. After they've spent more money on bags than most people in Las Vegas make in a week, they part ways, each stating they need to be somewhere else. Realizing this could be my chance, I wait for her to make her way from the store. My luck keeps getting better and better.

Fiona walks with determination, weaving in and out of the crowd, holding her shopping bags close. Her toned body is impossible to ignore, her skirt is skimming just below her round ass, and her tank top is completely cut out in the back, indicating there's no bra under there. I can't help but to ogle her as I saunter through the crowd myself, finally stopping as she enters a coffee shop. Before going in, I wait.

She orders a caramel latte and takes a seat farthest away from the window, tucking her newly purchased items against the wall. I go in and inhale deeply, even though I don't need to. I love the smell of coffee, and I tend to make one at home from time to time, just to enjoy the scent as it reminds me of a cross between vanilla beans and fresh soil. There's something lovely about it, and it's a smell that's been around for as long as I can remember.

With a cup of black coffee in my hand, I seek out the

empty seat next to her. "Is this seat taken?" I ask in a smooth tone.

When her eyes meet mine, I feel as though I'm being compelled for just a moment. The icy blue color shines right through me as she looks up from her book. "Um, no. Please help yourself." She motions at the chair before turning her attention back to her novel.

Taking the seat next to her, I see what she's reading, but am unfamiliar with the words, and by chance, the title on the page is covered. Everything about her is too perfect. Her nails, makeup, and hair. Her vain superficiality turns my stomach, but I remind myself I have a goal to accomplish, and it's to find myself in her favor. Regardless of how human she is.

"You look familiar; have we met?" I ask.

Looking annoyed at the interruption, she replies without looking at me again. "I don't believe so."

Becoming further frustrated with her disinterest, I continue. "I'm certain that we have. Aren't you hosting the party this weekend for casino investors?"

Now that I've piqued her interest, she sets her book down and attempts to turn on her business charm. Her eyes move over me as she tries to remember where we've met before. "My apologies, but I don't recall meeting you. Are you planning to attend the event?" She forms a fake smile.

"I am hoping to attend, yes."

"Well, that will be lovely, Mr....?"

"Roman." I hold my hand out to her, watching her body language shift when she feels the cold of my touch. As if on cue, she reaches up to fondle the cross that dangles at her neck.

"Mr... Roman," she repeats quietly. She's intriguing, watching my every move, studying me. I already know she's never had contact with a vampire directly, that she's aware of, so this encounter, friendly and short, is just enough. I've left my first impression, and stand to take leave.

"I'll see you this weekend, Miss Weston." I leave her sitting there without another glance. Only when I look back, she's still touching her neck. My distaste for humans like her has not waned, regardless of her beauty. She judges me without knowing anything at all, and for that, I shall take what I need from her. Within reason, of course.

The next task on my agenda is to secure an invitation to her event where I'll make my next move. Vampires are so well connected in every city, I easily could've arranged the invitation without meeting her to begin with, but planting the seed of intrigue is far more seductive than following her like a puppy at her event trying to meet her for the first time. As I leave the mall, I shut out everything around me, and focus on the sound of her rapid heartbeat.

The night air is stifling, yet there's something about the desert I'm starting to love. Brown has never been my color, but mix it with the red and orange of the sun, and it's quickly become a shade I can appreciate. Don't get me wrong, I'm counting the days until I can return to California, where I can dip my toes into the ocean and relax on the beach with enough of a breeze to keep me cool. This hot, tepid place is bad for my overall sense of being.

I turn and rest my elbows on the railing of my balcony. The glass doors separating the inside of my penthouse from my terrace are open, at least for the time being. Once fall arrives, I'll have them open more so I can enjoy the somewhat cooler temperatures. Right now though, they have to remain shut. The last thing I want is for my guests to feel uncomfortable while I'm trying to sell them on everything Las Vegas has to offer.

One of the event planners finishes stringing the last of the white lights, while the other members of the staff simultaneously pop open the many champagne bottles needed to create the fountain I had to have. It's frivolous, but Daddy's paying and only the best will suffice when it comes to his checkbook.

Inside, soft music plays through the surround sound, setting the right type of ambiance. I turn the dial down one notch, satisfied with the decibel level. Too loud and people can't think properly. Too quiet and you can hear each other's conversations from across the room. Neither are moments I want to happen, especially tonight. Everything has to be perfect. My father is counting on one of the influential investors to pad his pockets with the purchase of the Majesty. I'll receive a bonus, of course, and likely a European trip if I can seal the deal on the adjacent property as well.

Excusing myself, I slip into my bedroom and change rather quickly. Thankfully, my personal shopper does her job well and has an assortment of cocktail dresses for me to wear. I step into a little black sequins number with a scoop neck and no back. Moving from side to side in front of the mirror, I admire the way I look and start pulling my hair up and putting it back down, depending on which way I'm standing, to decide what style I like best. I finally decide on a half up, half down look, glancing over my shoulder to make sure enough of my back is showing. This, by far, is one of my favorite dresses. I make a mental note to ask my gal to buy more from this designer.

Tonight, we'll pretend we're all friends, having dinner and drinks, and sharing a casual conversation. The only business discussions taking place will be the subtle hints I drop about what my father's looking for. Mostly cash, but he's not above taking cars, boats and lakefront properties.

As I come out of my room, my doorman is opening the door. The first of the investors are here. Everything about them, I have memorized. From their faces, names, wives, and husbands, children, and their businesses. I know who's banging their secretary, whose wife has a hot cabana boy, and whose side piece is pregnant. Pregnancy is always a bigger scandal than an affair. I march forward with authority. My hand's extended and instantly in Ginger Madhu's hand, shaking it firmly. Ginger's husband, Frederic, kisses me on both cheeks. I can't stand him. He uses Ginger for her money, and because of this, I often refer to him as Fred, which he absolutely hates. He likes to pretend he's French when he's really from some small town in Oklahoma. He forgets I know everything.

"Ginger, I'm so happy you could make it."

"I wouldn't have missed the chance to put my bid in." She turns as the elevator dings. Out step Richard and Tara Bolton, Nevada's self-proclaimed royal family. Tara rushes toward Ginger and embraces her. If Tara had a knife, she'd likely start stabbing Ginger while telling her how much she loves her.

"Richard, so good of you to make it." He kisses me on my cheek and whispers into my ear, telling me how sexy I am. Pig. "Tara!" I step out of Richard's grasp and hold my arms out for his wife to come toward me. She smiles, but it's forced, and the hug she gives is cold. There's definitely something wrong, but now isn't the time to figure it out. Maybe she's pissed I was able to score the new Louis bag the second it hit the shelf.

"I just love... well, I thought you'd change the décor since the last time we were here," Tara says as she all but pushes me aside to enter my home. I do everything I can to keep from rolling my eyes. Richard snickers beside me, tapping my ass as he walks by me. Like I said, he's a pig, and I hate having him in my home. Thankfully, with a house full of people and a staff, he won't be able to try anything.

"I'll add it to my list of things to accomplish before my next dinner party." As much as I don't want to change the décor in my house to appease her, I will. The last thing I need or want is for her to talk about me among our mutual friends. If words get back to my father, he'll be rather upset with me for not satisfying his clients.

The elevator dings before I have a chance to make my way into the living room where the two couples are. Heath and Elaine McLeod walk through my door and embrace me in a tight hug. They're Lana's parents and here for moral support. Every time they hear about one of these dinners, they invite themselves. I don't mind because I appreciate having someone here I can talk to without having to be fake or discuss business.

"Thank you for coming." Elaine's the closest person I have to a mother with my own gallivanting across the country, mending a broken heart for the past ten, or is it fifteen, years. After eight, I stopped counting, stopped caring. My father may be the worst, but he didn't abandon me.

"We wouldn't miss it. Besides, your view is amazing, and I wanted to capture a few images tonight." Elaine pats the camera bag she's carrying. Heath's a doctor, while Elaine's a photographer. Her prints garner four to five digits, and if you're thinking about booking her for a wedding, think again. She's booked solid for a year.

The last to arrive are Shan Caldwell and his date, who's wearing some string dress and platform stripper shoes. This time, my eyes roll when he stops and sticks his tongue down her throat, and his hand slides up her leg, exposing her ass. I've known Shan for most of my life, and at one point our parents wanted us to get married. I probably would've taken the plunge, but Shan's wandering eye and inability to keep his hands to himself are a huge turnoff to me. Call me old-fashioned, but when I marry, it'll be for love and not business.

"Fiona," Shan drags my name out as his kiss lingers all too close to my lips.

"Shan. I see you brought the best of Vegas with you. Let me guess, you woke up with her in your bed?" I keep my eyes on the woman, who is chomping on her gum like a cow chews its cud. He turns and extends his hand to her.

"This is Tiffany Desiree."

"And what corner do you work on?" I'm not ashamed of my question. I'm totally judging her by the way she's dressed and how handsy he is with her. Clearly, she doesn't understand my insulting question by the look on her face. "Right, welcome." I motion for Shan and his friend to go into the living room. The only other people who could possibly stop by are Lana or my father. Usually, my father won't attend these functions because he looks culpable in the solicitation of gifts.

More people arrive. They're either associates of my father or friends of his new wife. Either way, it doesn't bother me. The larger the audience, the better the outcome. There is always someone who wants to outdo their competition.

The drinks are flowing. My champagne fountain seems to be a hit, especially with Tiffany, and the staff has put out our dinner. I stand back and watch the investors meander in and out of my library where I conveniently have the Majesty on display, along with the potential earnings if the remodel is done right. The Majesty is one of the rare properties in Vegas where expansion is possible.

"What's your father looking for?" Shan asks as he comes to stand next to me on the balcony.

"I don't know what you're talking about."

He leans his arms on the railing and nods. "I was at the car show the other day, came across the Lambo Huracan. I put a down payment on it. I was thinking of ordering two."

I nod. "Probably a good idea."

Shan brings his drink to his lips and swallows the rest of his Scotch. He leaves me there, knowing the price my father is willing to accept to streamline the permitting process. What would normally take years, he will make happen in days. Suddenly, when one of these applications crosses his desk, he's not very busy and can make things happen rather quickly.

I step back into my house and watch the people I've invited into my home. They mingle among themselves, talking business and setting plans to get together for their imaginary golf games. As I look over the crowd, there's a set of blue eyes, which do not belong here.

Walking through the crowd takes me longer than I intend with people stopping and talking to me.

"How'd you get in?" I ask, meeting his gaze. I'm taken aback by his strong jawline, which is covered in the perfect amount of stubble. I find this feature extremely attractive. My fingers itch to run through it, to feel his coarse hair tickle my skin. The rest of him looks perfect as if he were cut out of Vogue and set in the middle of my room to entice me with his broad shoulders and his visible physique. However, it's his already sexed, roughed up looking hair that garners my attention or is it his mesmerizing blue eyes? Maybe a combination of both? Doesn't matter because I didn't invite him here.

Even though he has a glass of bourbon in his hand, he doesn't take a drink. Most often, men will do this when approached by women. It's their way of mustering up the courage to speak to the opposite sex. Yet, he holds it between his thumb and index finger, letting the amber liquid slosh back and forth. Odd, but his choice to ruin a perfectly fine liquor.

"The door was open?"

"Not likely," I tell him, crossing my arms over my chest. I wrack my brain, trying to recall his name, but to no avail. This is unlike me. I pride myself on remembering everything about everyone. "Try again?"

This time, he brings the glass to his lips, and that's when I see it, the Mark of the Fates. I step back, wondering why I didn't notice this when we met. Instantly, I reach for my cross, only to find it's not hanging around my neck. He notices but doesn't budge, but his eyes meet mine. I don't know what compulsion feels like, and I'm not willing to find out. "Excuse me."

I leave him standing there and rush to my room. All I want is my necklace. Once it's securely around my neck, I turn to find the vampire standing in my doorway. I swallow hard and try to stand tall, but my legs wobble in my stilettos. "Please leave."

"I'm not here to hurt you."

"Then why are you here?" I can feel my pulse throbbing, and I imagine he can see it pushing through my skin, beckoning him to come sink his teeth into my flesh.

"To talk business."

"We don't do business with your kind."

The vampire steps into my room and closes the door behind him. I could scream, but he'd likely kill me, turn into a bat and fly away with my body. My luck, he'd leave me in the desert for the wild animals to eat me, once he's drained me of my blood. "Please don't." I hold my hands up and back away slowly, but he steps back and leans against the door.

"I'm asking for five minutes. I'm not here to hurt you, suck your blood or kill anyone at your party. I'm here to talk business. I'm a legitimate businessman looking to break into the Vegas market."

I square my shoulders and muster up all the courage I have. "My father doesn't do business with vampires. I suggest you take your money to a state that favors your kind. Nevada isn't it. Now get out of my house." I point and stomp my foot for emphasis.

5

ROMAN

*H*er lips purse as she examines me, and I can't tell if she's scared or if she's pissed off.

"My father doesn't do business with vampires. I suggest you take your money to a state that favors your kind. Nevada isn't it. Now get out of my house." My kind. I refrain from rolling my eyes as if we haven't walked the earth for hundreds of years in secret.

Raising my hands in mock surrender, I smile and relax against the door of her bedroom. "Listen, I have more money than all of those plastic faced, cheating, liars combined. Give me a chance to talk about my plans, and let's just pretend for a moment that we're two people, which we are, just talking business. You don't even know me." Assaying her face, I can see that she is at least mildly intrigued by me. After all, I'm not showing fangs, I look like any other normal guy for the most part, and I'm certainly not threatening.

Although her shoulders relax slightly, and she stands a bit taller, she's firm. "You need to leave. There's no way my father is going to give you what you're looking for, so you're wasting your time."

Part of her wants me to stay; I can sense it. Her fingertips fondle the cross that she wears for protection, and while it doesn't have any real power, and couldn't stop me from physically doing anything, I respect it. I know I need a new plan, and I decide to retreat and regroup before there's any kind of scene. I'm unclear how her guests feel about doing business with a vampire, but I suspect they all have similar views.

"I'm sorry to hear that, Fiona. I'm not what you think, and I wish you'd give me the chance to show you who I really am."

"I know who you really are..." she trails off.

"Roman. My name is Roman," I reply softly.

"Roman," she repeats under her breath.

While her intrigue is evident, it's also clear that it's time to go. "I hope to cross paths with you again, Fiona," I say, swiftly leaving the room and making my way out of her penthouse. It appears that no one noticed her absence, or noticed me at all, which is how I prefer it to be. Dejected, but determined, I head to Clutch to eat and see if I can come up with a new plan.

Clutch is an elite club, catering to vampires specifically. While there are plenty of humans about, and most of the bartenders are mortal, the clientele consists of vampires and humans. It is a place where we can be ourselves. Humans are only permitted if they agree to the terms of Clutch policies, which mostly involves volunteering themselves physically for feeding us. There's usually a degree of sexual pleasure involved as well, but that's not why I'm going. I'm hungry, and I need to think.

As a regular there, I don't need to show my mark to get in. In fact, the doorman Corban and I have known each other for many years, and he waves me right in.

"Sir," he says as I approach.

"Stop calling me that. It's ridiculous." I shake my head at his formality.

Grinning, he shows his fangs are out. "Just doing my job, mate." He lets out a chuckle. His pale skin, the same color as mine, shines with a bit of a red glow from the neon light above us.

"Yeah, yeah. Is Selene here?"

"She is indeed. She's always here, mate." Corban's slight Australian accent has always been something I was jealous of. It was easy to get the ladies as a vampire, but a vampire with an accent, now that was something special. I'd never had an accent except for the brief time I spent in England. I somehow picked up a bit of a British one at the time, and still somewhat enjoyed using some of their euphemisms.

"Thanks, brother. I'll catch up with you later. I need to eat."

"There are plenty of delicious morsels to feast on tonight my friend. Mmhmm." He licks his lips. He feeds far more than he needs to, mostly because it's offered to him on a silver platter by merely working here.

With a grin and a nod, I pass by, entering the club. I think it's much like one would expect a vampire club to look. There's a fair amount of red velvet and black curtains everywhere, and while much of it resembles a typical night-club, there's an innate sensual vibe in the room. The room has a husky sounding trance mix, not fast enough to dance to, but too rhythmic to be considered mellow. Heightened senses give me the ability to smell and hear the humans, tucked away into dark corners, letting their bodies be used as fuel for us. It's as if it were always meant to be, humans and vampires coexisting. It is a place where I feel comfortable, among my people, and those who choose to accept and enjoy us.

While it may seem vile or taboo to some, the natural connection between a vampire and a human in these circumstances is quite beautiful. The human receives pleasure. So enjoyable, they tend to come back for more time and again. The joy can be kind of a pure necessity, but it can also be extremely sexual in nature, as tends to be the case most often. Yes, it's a bite, and yes, the human's blood is consumed, but the intimacy involved can be quite erotic. In fact, making love, or simply fucking when you are feeding, can be amazing for everyone involved. All of these are allowed at the club so long as permission is granted, which is the point of places like this. The vampire, of course, receives food, replenishment. We don't have to feed often, but we do have to feed. The connection is magical under the right circumstances, and in my lifetime I've come upon a human every now and again who I want to pleasure and to feed on more often than just what's necessary. It's been a long time since then though.

I know I need to find sustenance for myself tonight, but I need to find Selene first and discuss my options for what I should do next. She is not only the owner of Clutch, but has been a friend, business partner, and a confidante since I became a vampire. We traveled the world together for more time than I can even recall, and we also chose to settle ourselves in Las Vegas at the same time as well.

It doesn't take me long to find her, behind the bar, talking to some human men who are fawning over her. Vampires are beautiful, and she's no exception. She notices me immediately, and as I approach, she dismisses the disappointed gentlemen hoping to be hers for the evening.

"And to what do I owe the pleasure of your company tonight? You must be hungry." She smiles, adding a wink for good measure. "I can find one for you unless you have your eyes set on something in particular?" She waves a perfectly manicured hand at the room.

"I do need something, but first, I need to talk. I have a situation."

She leans over the bar, getting comfortable, ready to listen. "That sounds dramatic, Roman. Let's hear it."

"You know that I'm trying to buy that old casino, right?"

She nods. "Yes, you never did tell me why you want that old dump."

"That's not important. What's important is that the gaming commission won't do business with vampires. And, I can't get my gaming license without it, which means I can't buy the casino without it."

Rolling her eyes, she groans. "These humans. I swear to you, Roman. I miss the days where we took what we wanted. I'd rather hide in the shadows and have what I want than pander to these mere mortals. Who do they think they are?"

"If we were hiding in the shadows still, would you have this club? Would you be feeding on one... or will it be all three of those men tonight?" I raise an eyebrow at her. She's well known for her appetite - in blood, and in men.

"Hmph. Always the voice of reason, Roman. So what do you intend to do about this situation of yours? You're obviously not planning to give up, I see. What do you have in mind? I can smell the gears turning."

"Well, there's this woman..."

She interrupts me with a laugh. "Ha! Of course, there is."

"It's not like that. I mean... no, it's not like that at all."

"Okay, so tell me what it is like exactly." Her lips curl as she sarcastically awaits my explanation.

"The gaming commissioner's daughter. I think she can help me. But she's never been around us before. In fact, I'm fairly certain that I'm the first vampire she's ever even had a conversation with."

"Was she wearing a cross, Roman?" Selene stands upright again, crossing her arms.

"Well yes, but..."

"But what... you know the rules. You can't compel her. And far be it from me to tout the rules, but they are what they are." In the early days, Selene wasn't one to play by the rules much, but over the years, she has enjoyed the perks of walking among the humans as much as the rest of us. Her love of free feeding without all the messy hunting and her love of beautiful things like shopping and fancy shoes has toned down the huntress in her substantially.

Frustrated, I sigh. "I'm not planning to compel her exactly. I thought I might actually win her over."

"Win her over? You're planning to what... court her?"

I rub my chin thoughtfully; I like the sound of that. Courting. Like in the old days. Perhaps it's what Miss Fiona Weston needs, to be courted. "Yes. Court her. That's exactly what I'll do."

"How bad do you want this casino, Roman? You're treading in some dangerous water crossing the gaming board by what, bedding his daughter? Is that really the route you want to go?" She knows me well enough to know there's more to the story. She's waiting for me to tell her what it is.

"I want the casino. It's important. I have plans for it, and for the money it will generate."

"And?" she prods.

"And what?" I reply, pretending we're not going down this road.

"Let me guess. She's beautiful?"

"Well sure, she's pretty."

"Cut to the chase, Roman. I have things to do. I love you, but you should just tell me what the hell is really going on besides you trying to buy a casino you don't even need." Her hand moves firmly to her hip as her tone turns stern.

"Okay, okay," I concede. "Selene, there's something about her. I'm drawn to her, even though I rather loathe her life. She has this superficial, artificial lifestyle, but I can sense there's so much more."

"More than how delicious it would be to get her to take off the cross she wears?"

"Far more delicious, Selene. I can tell there's something in her that I need to know. And while yes, it'll help me get my casino, she's a mystery. Not only to someone like me but her friends as well. I watched her interact with them this evening; they haven't a clue who she truly is. And neither do I, but I want to find out."

Selene looks at me thoughtfully for a moment before she replies. "Roman, I have been your friend for hundreds of years. I've never once heard you say something like this about a human."

Surprising even myself with what I said, I nod. "I know."

"Well, then you should invest some time in it. Explore what draws you in. But you need to be careful. You don't need any trouble from the human government. That only causes trouble in ours. There's no happily ever after for humans and vampires; that's a fairy tale, so don't forget it."

As I consider what she's said, I realize that while she may be right, I don't care. Even just a few moments I'd spent in her bedroom, inhaling her scent, listening to her heartbeat, left me wanting more.

6

FIONA

*T*he bags under my eyes have bags under theirs. No amount of lifting, pulling or tugging seems to negate any of the swellings. "Stupid vampire," I mutter to the mirror. I apply a heavy dose of the cream I had the bellhop bring up, and fan my face, hoping it dries quickly and works like magic. This is going to be a sunglass day, and I'll have to pretend I'm hungover, even though I barely had one glass of champagne.

I blame the stupid vampire. If it weren't for him, my party would've been a hit. Oh, who am I kidding, the party was still a success, minus the few minutes the one known as Roman made his presence known.

Actually, he didn't do anything to make himself stand out. He minded his own business, and truthfully, if I hadn't met him the other day at the café, I probably wouldn't have even noticed him. Nevertheless, he was in my home, holding a glass of bourbon, which I now know he didn't drink, watching me as if I were his prey. The thought makes me shudder, except not in the way it should. I should be disgusted, repulsed and feeling violated. This... thing entered my home, uninvited, and followed me to the safe haven of my bedroom. Yet, all I can think about is what Lana so graciously divulged about her locker room happenings, and how being with a vampire was the best sex she's ever had, and well... let me just say it's been a while and I found myself turned on by his bravado.

I didn't handle myself professionally at all. It's not like he'll call my father and file a complaint, but it's still unsettling to me. My friends, without my consent, could do business with him, and he could tarnish my name. If he did, I'd deserve it. After all, I'm the hostess. It's my job to bring the investors together, even if they have no right buying property.

My cross rests right at the peak of my breast. I pick it up, twisting it a few times before letting it fall on my bare skin. As far as I know, it's never failed me before, but again, I could be completely naïve. I've been told I'm not the most observant, which is evident by the fact I let this Roman speak to me yesterday. Where was his mark the other day in the coffee shop? Had he hidden it from me or was I not looking?

"You weren't looking," I say to myself. I wasn't because I was so taken by how handsome he is and how distinguished he presented himself. Most often, the men who hit on me are college-aged preppy boys looking for a good time. But then again, all vampires are gorgeous, and it's clear I can't make a decision between fact and fiction.

Fact, I didn't sleep well last night because each time I closed my eyes, Roman was there, hovering over me, making me feel things I have never felt. He was soft, nothing like the rock hard façade we're led to believe these creatures have.

Fiction, I imagined he called his penis Vlad the Impaler before he jabbed me with it. Yes, jabbed!

Fact, I had my first wet dream. I soaked my panties, dreaming about Roman.

Fiction, when he opened his mouth, his fangs fell out, stabbing me in the heart.

Fact, Roman smells divine, and if I inhale deeply, I can still smell his lingering scent. I don't know if all vamps smell the same or if the warm sand fragrance is from his cologne.

Rifling through my jewelry box, I find the last gift my mother gave me, diamond cross earrings. I used to think they were gaudy, but right now I could use all the extra help I can muster. The cross is supposed to keep them away, prevent them from compelling us. It's supposed to be a bright red beacon letting every one of them know we're off limits.

Once again, my hand reaches for my cross, only this time it ghosts over my breast. I close my eyes, only to picture Roman's hand doing the work, tweaking my nipples until they're hard and ready. My eyes flash open, and I tear my hand away from my body. I shudder at the thought of a vampire bringing me this much pleasure.

Right now, I hate Lana. If it weren't for her and her gym hook-up, I'd never have these fantasies. I blame her and her big mouth. What she does in private should stay there. She doesn't need to be a tabloid and share every detail with her friends.

Except, it's what we do. Well, Leslie doesn't.

And I hate the fact that I need another pair of clean underwear. Stupid vampire.

As LUCK WOULD HAVE IT, Lana and Leslie want to meet at the spa. I agreed, only because I couldn't think of a lie strong enough to keep them away from my penthouse. If I were to say I was sick, they'd both show up with soup. If I told them I was meeting someone else, they'd hound me until I came clean or searched all over Las Vegas until they found me. My friends may be a little unhinged. It was only after I agreed to meet them, under the strict stipulation they weren't to fight about anything, did they say we had a full day of spa services ahead of us. Truthfully, I need this, but answering questions as to why luggage tagged eyes read international, isn't going to be fun.

Yet, here I am waiting in the lobby wearing my biggest pair of sunglasses with the lifeguard staring at me. I peg him to be about seventeen or eighteen, and he's finding some reason to continue to come to the front desk. Each time, he stands there, as if he's waiting for a client to come in.

Luckily for me, he can't see the eye roll I give him each time he spreads his arms out along the counter. I mean, the kid is openly gawking, and I feel like I'm about to vomit. I look down at my watch to see the time. Lana and Leslie are both late, which is unlike them. After the other day, I can't imagine they would arrive together, but for all I know they kissed and made up, which would be ideal. I don't want my two best friends not getting along. It doesn't bode well for me.

Finally, they walk in. Leslie is yammering away on her phone, while Lana looks happy as can be. She kisses me on both cheeks because rich people have to act European.

"How was your party?"

"Good, great turn out as usual. I'm sure Daddy will be very happy. Oh, Shan was there. He brought a stripper."

Lana's mouth drops open. "Seriously?"

I nod and motion toward Leslie, who is standing in the corner, still on her phone. Lana shrugs. "Who's she talking to?"

"David? Bob? Jeremy? Honestly, I don't know who she's dating right now."

"Wait, what happened to Larry?"

"You mean Laurence?" Lana draws the middle of his name out in some phony accent. I nod.

"Doesn't fit Daddy's financial bio, so she dumped him."

"Wow."

"The trust fund is everything." Lana's right. To some it is. "Anyway, Shan and a stripper?"

"No joke. I can't imagine what his mother is thinking." Shan's mother is the definition of elitist. She was born into money, married into more money, and when her father died, she inherited even more. I'm not sure Shan's mother has worked a day in her life.

"But it was good to see him?"

I shrug. "It was fine. He wants to work with Daddy, which is the only reason we dated, to begin with."

"What's with the shades?" Leslie asks.

I feel about two feet tall under her scrutiny. She's always perfect. Never has a hair out of place, a broken nail or chipped polish.

Before I can answer, one of our technicians calls our names. We follow her down the hall, passing the pool where the creepy teenage lifeguard is watching. "Weirdo."

"Who?" Leslie asks.

"I'll tell you later." As much as his staring bothered me, I don't want to get him into trouble. For some, what he was doing is flattery. The young man only needs to hone his skills a bit better, maybe not be so up front with the leering.

As soon as we enter the dressing room, I'm forced to

remove my glasses. Leslie makes a face, which tells me I'm really unbecoming.

Lana's eyes go wide. "Rough night? Shan ditch the hooker and come back?"

I shake my head. "No, nothing like that."

"Are you sick? Did you get your flu shot this year?" Leslie asks.

"I'm not sick. I didn't sleep well."

"Sex will do that to you."

"Lana, why is everything about sex?" Leslie asks with her hands on her hips. The only thing missing from her stance is having her foot jut out like a mother scorning her child.

Lana saunters over to Leslie, swaying her hips back and forth. "Don't knock it until you try it."

Leslie huffs. "I'm saving myself for marriage."

"But why? Don't you want to experience men before you settle on one?" Lana asks. "What if your husband doesn't know what he's doing? Or worse yet, what if you don't marry a virgin?" Lana scoffs and covers her mouth.

"Leave her alone, Lana," I say. "She has her reasons, and you do as well, so respect them. Same goes for you, Leslie." I go to both of them and place one arm on each of their shoulders.

"You're my best friends, I need you to get along."

"Are you going to tell us why you didn't sleep well?" Lana asks, crossing her arms over her chest.

I roll my eyes, angry for not canceling on them today. "No." I leave them standing in the dressing room. I smile at the woman doing my massage and lay face down on the table as she requests. Lana and Leslie are still bickering when they come, but quiet down as soon as they're on the table.

I'm quickly lost in the sensation of deft fingers working through the knots in my back. The push and pull lulls my eyes shut. Of course, all I can see is Roman, and it makes me wonder if he's put me under some spell. I know nothing about the... man? And yet I can't seem to stop thinking about him.

When I moan aloud, Lana hollers at me.

"Sorry," I mumble.

"Who's Roman?" she asks.

"Is he the reason you have bags under your eyes, Fiona, because I have to tell you, it's very unfitting, especially for a place like this," Leslie says so matter-of-factly. My God, this woman drives me insane. Please, someone, tell me why we're friends.

I turn my head to find both of them staring at me. Well, mostly Lana because she's right next to me, but I can feel Leslie's fiery gaze. "Where did you hear that name?"

"You were having a sex dream about him," Lana tells me.

"I was not." I rise up on my elbows and look at my masseuse. "Was I?"

She shrugs and starts working on my calves.

"Spill."

I look at Lana and lie back down. "I have nothing to say because nothing happened between us."

"But who is he?" she asks.

"He showed up at my party last night, uninvited."

"But who is he? Is he someone we know?" Leslie asks.

I look at Lana and silently plead for her help. Her eyes go wide, and I shake my head, but it's too late. Her mouth is already opening. "He's a vampire?"

"What?" Leslie screeches as she sits up. "Not you too, Fi."

"I didn't do anything. I swear. I asked him to leave, but now I can't get him off my mind."

Leslie hops down from the table and stalks over to me. She grabs my neck, rubbing up and down. "I said I wasn't with him."

"But you're having impure thoughts about him. He planted something on you."

"He never touched me," I tell her. My dreams don't count.

Leslie stands back; her towel is barely hanging on. "How would you know? They're lightning fast. He could've been super quick, and you would've never known it."

She's right, but there's something about Roman that makes me believe he's different, that he's not like the others we've read about or seen on the streets.

7

ROMAN

I contemplated what Selene said; explore what draws you. It was the perfect description of how I am feeling. Drawn to Fiona. She is a woman of many layers, who seems to be playing a part, most likely for her father. What I could sense of her when she was near me was more than just physical attraction, and I decide not to waste any time; I am going to find her and speak to her again. I'd intentionally left things open-ended between us so that this door was open to an extent, but I'd not had a plan until now.

I look in the usual spots my research has led me to, without much luck until finally, I can sense her. I can actually smell her. The scent reminds me of lilacs in the warm summer sun, and I try to recall where I smelled that before. As I follow the scent, my connection to her presence becomes stronger, and I can now hear her heartbeat. It's calm as if she's sleeping. When I realize that she is at a spa, I pick up the sounds of her annoying friends as well.

The ones named Lana and Leslie are with her, and from the sounds of it, they are having another conversation about vampires, which brings a broad grin to my face. If the topic is once again vampires then it seems I left an impression. I feel Fiona's heart rate increase, and I use my gifts to listen in on the ladies' conversation, which is now turning to be about me. This is far better than I'd imagined it would be. Once again, Leslie is lecturing everyone about how bad vampires are, and judging everyone's life choices. Such a trivial human experience.

I certainly cannot go talk to Fiona in the spa, with her friends around, that isn't the point of seeking her out today, so I find a spot nearby where I can focus, and hear what's being said. Listening to her speak, her voice like a smooth song, she talks of meeting me, and I cannot help but feel a sense of relief at the impression that I've left. Part of me had been nervous that she wouldn't have been taken with me at all, and I'd be back to square one with my business dealings, but even worse than that now was that I want her to like me. I want her to understand who I am, who my people are, and what we are about. Without the propaganda that's been planted into her head of course.

The ladies spend the entire day at the spa, and while some would say I could make better use of my time, this is the only thing I want to be doing. Once they finally finish their day of leisure, I wait to find out where she is going next so that I can finally talk to her. Because I listen to her all day, it almost feels as though we are having a conversation in some ways; I get to hear her voice what is on her mind, but she doesn't get to be privy my thoughts, which is almost unfair. Such is the plight of mortal man I suppose. Being a vampire is quite wonderful, except for those moments you're trying to convince a human you're not going to murder them. I could do without those moments.

Anyway, I continue to wait for the girls to part ways,

anticipating Fiona's next move. I hope she is going to the coffee shop.

"Bye girls, love you!" I hear her say as her footsteps approach. I'm waiting on the sidewalk near the spa, but just out of range for her friends to see me.

"Love you too! Text me later! Go see about a vampire, will ya?" the one named Lana shouts in the street, making me chuckle audibly. That Lana is funny, and Fiona should definitely keep her around. I do not hear the vampire-hating friend interject, and I can hear their two sets of footsteps going in the other direction. Perfect, she is alone.

As she turns the corner to where I'm standing, I try not to startle her, which is damn near impossible. "Fiona?" I say as non-threateningly as possible.

"Oh my God!" She jumps, clutching at her neck quickly. A bit dramatic, but there wasn't any way to surprise her without, well... surprising her.

"Fiona, relax. I didn't mean to startle you."

"Well then what the hell are you doing hiding out here?" she demands, panting.

"It's broad daylight. I wasn't really hiding," I offer.

She puts her hand on her hip, and tilts her head, scrutinizing me. "I suppose you're right. However, were you out here waiting for me?"

I want to lie and say I was randomly passing by, but we both know I was absolutely sitting out here waiting for her. "I was hoping that we could talk, just for a bit? Could I take you to lunch?"

Her face scrunches up, and she crosses her arms. "Lunch? Do you even eat?" She's skeptical of me, and I get it, but I'm not giving up.

"Well, not human food, but I'd be delighted to buy you food, and pretend to eat while we talk?" I offer.

Somehow, this elicits a smile from her, as if she's amused. "Yea, I'm not going to sit with you and have you watch me eat, that's weird."

"It's only weird if you care what other people think. Besides, I'll order food. I just won't eat it. Come on. I can tell you want to." I smile at her, tilting my head like a playful puppy.

Her shoulders relax, and she is still smiling. "All right. I'll let you buy me lunch. But I get to pick the place since I'm the only one eating," she declares with a light giggle.

"You got a deal, Ms. Weston. Shall we?" I step aside so that she will lead the way.

She walks past me, clutching her new Louis Vuitton with one arm, her other hand still floating near her neck, but it's drifted lower, closer to her breasts. I can't help but notice her beautiful curves. Her chest is of average size, but she has a perfect hourglass figure, accentuated by her skin tight jeans which draw my eyes directly to her ass. The more I'm around her, the closer I want to get to her, but she's still scared of me. I need to show her that I'm really just a man in the most important ways.

"I am in the mood for a Greek salad, and there is a place not too far from here. Will that work?" she asks.

"Sounds fantastic." In my human life, I never had Greek food, but I have been to Greece as a vampire. It's a beautiful country, with extraordinarily beautiful people. The human violence in the last 100 years became a turn off for me, which is why I left.

THE RESTAURANT HAS a small symbol on the front of the building, next to the fire department signs. It is the symbol that I carry on my wrist. She's chosen an establishment that welcomes vampires, which is not lost on me and endears me to her further. All public buildings are required to welcome vampires, but human-owned businesses are not required to serve vampires if they do not wish, and establishments that do welcome us openly often display the sticker on their door as a sign of acceptance.

Once we are seated, she orders her salad, and I do the same. I then jump right into what I want to say. "Have you looked at my business proposal?" I ask.

"No, I haven't," she admits. "I don't tend to read all of them to be completely honest, as many of them are a real bore, and are primarily about who can get the best deal to make more money. I just do my job, which is to gather the money together, so they all know who has some, and who's in the market to spend some of theirs on an investment."

"Tell me about your father."

"Why?"

"Because I would like to understand him better," I reply frankly.

"Understanding him better is not going to get you a deal. He's not going to work with a vampire, Roman. There's really no way around that." Our salads arrive, and she begins to pick at hers while I watch.

"I didn't say anything about that. I would genuinely like to better understand the man. You seem to be open to me in some ways, so why not him?" Her face flushes immediately, and I can sense that she is embarrassed that I notice. Unsure of what to say, I wait patiently for her reply.

"My daddy simply doesn't understand your kind, Roman, and honestly, I can't say that I do either. You frighten me. But I'm willing to admit, that is because of folklore and what I've heard from my father. It just feels like bigotry or a reason to hate you without cause, and that's not who I am as a person." She seems like she wants to say more; she fidgets in her seat a bit, looking uncomfortable.

"It is not my intent to frighten you, Fiona. In fact, it's quite the opposite." I feel a smirk begin to form as I shamelessly flirt, just a bit. Watching her turn red is fast becoming a huge turn on for me.

She takes a breath before replying, collecting her thoughts. "I can see that you are actually a nice... man." She pauses. "But I honestly do not think that I can help you. My influence is minimal, and my father isn't going to change his tune about vampires. He's old-fashioned and set in his ways."

"Perhaps you can read my proposal. I will email it to you, and then if you don't think it's worth anything, I will walk away or find myself a human to partner with as I've been instructed to do. But I want you to read it."

"Why me? I told you, I'm just the party girl. I just hook people up like a matchmaker."

"Fiona, you're so much more than the party girl." She blushes again, and lowers her chin, looking up at me through her lashes. Her blue eyes bore into me, and at this moment I want to tell her all about my plans, but I don't. I reach across the small table, extending my finger out under her chin. As I gently lift her chin, so she looks at me directly, her warm skin sends electricity through me. Heat engulfs my skin, a sensation I've not felt for as long as I can remember. I can hear her heartbeat pick up again as if it's beating in my own chest. Possibly a dash of fear, but definitely something else. "I want to know what you think of it. I want your opinion on my proposal, and then I want you to tell me that you don't want to help me."

She replies softly. "I will look at it. But I cannot make you any promises."

"Just promise that I can see you again. So that we can... talk more." I hesitate, my growing attraction to her making me want to sweep her into my arms, taking her back to my place for safe keeping. Her soft smile exposes her beauty; she's herself with me. Not at all the woman who I thought she'd be.

Shyly, she replies. "That... I can promise." Her expression is inviting; a smile that begins to melt my exterior spreads across her face.

And with that, I lower my hand and sit back in my seat. With Fiona, I need to be patient. I need to ensure that she's not scared of me and that she allows me to get a bit closer each time we meet. Anything more, and I could lose her, and I can't bear the thought of that.

8

FIONA

*T*he words start to blur. It doesn't matter how many times I read them. Each time I come to the part of Roman's proposal where he wants to open a home not only serving homeless people but more importantly the foster children of Las Vegas. I can't wrap my head around why a vampire would want to help humans. None of this makes sense to me.

A few times while reading, I picked up my phone to call him because I had to know, but I could never bring myself to dial his number. Right now, I hate myself for thinking about him outside of a business standpoint. He's nothing more than a client. No, he's not even a client. He's someone who doesn't take no for an answer, and as much as I'd love to sell this idea to my father, and beg him to give Roman the permits necessary, my father would never budge. Roman doesn't have the right vital organs.

However, the concept is beyond amazing and needs to happen, and if Roman needs to find a human partner to make this project come to life then, that's what he needs to do. I wish I could tell him this, but the other day at lunch he didn't seem too keen on the idea of having a human involved in his business, not that I blame him. After we parted, I stopped at the library and did some research on vampires. The first thing I learned, despite their extraordinary abilities, is humans have always somehow had control. At one point in history, more vampires walked the earth than humans, yet we were responsible for the extinction of the undead. It's not exactly clear why the reemergence happened, but that the government has put strict guidelines on vampires' ability to walk among us.

Their rules are simple, to say the least. While the cross I wear doesn't protect me, the vampire is supposed to respect it, which Roman has done each time we've met. The books also stated there are rogue members out there who do as they wish, but a majority of the creations are trying to live among humans, as humanly as possible.

Still, as much as I like this proposal, the only way Roman achieves his goal is to hand it over to a human. I'm fairly sure my father won't even entertain the idea if a vampire is involved, even as a silent partner.

Holding one of his architectural sketches in my hand, I lean back in my chair. The new home is perfect for the empty lot, is beautiful and nothing like we have on the Strip. Even though it would have the same grandiose feel as the casinos or stores along the road, it fits. Truthfully, when I opened the portfolio, I expected to find a gothic vibe, with pages filled with black, coffins and cobwebs. I blame my father for my thought process.

Roman is nothing like I had imagined, and it makes me wonder what type of human he was before he was... what do they call it? Turned? Bitten? The book I read didn't exactly go into detail of how someone becomes a vampire, and something tells me his creator didn't bite him because he was dying of Spanish influenza when he was seventeen. I can attest, Roman doesn't sparkle, but he does dazzle me, and part of me hates it. As Leslie says, it's unnatural, but I'd be a liar if I said I haven't thought about Roman since our lunch date. I have, in every possible way. It's that part of me that wants to know him more, to find out what makes him tick and discover why this project is so important to him. He could go any place else and build something like this, so why Vegas?

As much as I want to help him, I can't. There isn't anything I can do. Knowing this breaks my heart because Roman seems to be more kind than his human counterparts. The other proposals are just money making ventures. Investors looking to dump millions into a failing hotel, making it a hot spot for the next year while collecting copious amounts of revenue and eventually letting it fall by the wayside as the current owners have. No one considers the long-term investment. They're unprepared for the complaints that will undoubtedly come in about the air conditioner not working, the uncomfortable bed, dirty room or the loud banging coming from their adjacent wall. Each of these items cost money, and unless you're jam-packing your casino, the hotel is going to struggle.

Did Roman consider this? I don't know why I care, but I rifle through his proposal to see. My eyes scan the page, and sure enough, he has. He has the funds to do a complete overhaul of the current hotel, upgrading it to the finest of everything the market has to offer, all while keeping his prices competitive, if not below market.

"Why can't everyone think like him?"

When did I start thinking of Roman as a pronoun? I still don't know the answer. Is he a man? He looks like, talks like, and acts like – well better than some, I know – a man. So why not? And if he's not, what do I call him?

I shouldn't call him anything. In a matter of days, this... whatever he is, has entered my home uninvited, stalked me outside the spa I was enjoying the day at with my friends, and... that's when it hits me. He approached me in the coffee shop, knowing who I was. It wasn't happenstance or a shy flirtation, he sought me out with the sole purpose of getting to know me because of who my father is. With that, I close his portfolio and tuck it into my desk drawer, determined to forget it.

I DON'T KNOW how I ended up here, but here I am, standing in the middle of the Majesty Hotel and Casino, watching as very few people push quarters into the slot machines. As casinos go, this one is empty. The typically loud and boisterous sounds that represent Las Vegas do not exist here. At one time, the Majesty was a staple of the Strip, the hot spot mecca until misguided fortunes and super casinos opened.

"I hate my imaginary job."

"Cocktail?" A young... no strike that, he's not young because he's a vampire, is smiling at me. He's carrying an empty tray with a pad of paper on it.

"You're a vampire," I say, stupidly. I'm sure he knows this.

His expression changes as he looks around. "If you're uncomfortable, I can ask Jenny to come take your order."

I shake my head. "I'm sorry for my outburst, it was rude of me."

Now he steps back as his eyes go wide. He opens his mouth to say something but quickly closes it. He clears his throat, which brings up another list of questions I have. Like, do vampires go to school to learn how to act human or do they retain these mannerisms once they've turned? I'm sure Roman would answer anything I want to know, but honestly, I think seeing him is a bad idea. He makes me feel things, which I'm not sure are entirely true to the way I'm feeling. I'm convinced Roman has me under some spell or something.

"Do I have to gamble to get a drink?"

The waiter shrugs. "It's normally the rule, but the owners bend it."

"What do you mean?"

"Over the years, the owners have been very lax on the requirement. We can serve anyone free drinks."

"I see." This explains why they're losing so much money. Liquor sales, combined with gambling are what keep the casino afloat. The more people drink, the more they spend at the tables and slots. "I'm going to sit over there." I point behind me to the Wheel of Fortune machine. "I'll take a vodka sprint, please."

He smiles and tells me he'll be right back. I do as I told him and sit down at the machine. I've never been one to gamble, but today seems like a good day to let off some steam by punching the buttons as hard as I can. I feed the machine a twenty and start playing. Every few turns I win a dollar or two. It's enough to keep me in my seat, and before I know it, I've put more money into the machine and am on my third or fourth drink.

The more I drink, the louder I get when I hit the smallest of victories. I have no doubt my antics are the high-light of the security team watching me because when I lose,

I all but fall out of my chair and flail about like a fish without water.

"No whammies," I yell, pushing the button down. I figure if I hold it longer my electronic spin will be more powerful.

"Ma'am, the no whammies machine is over there. I can show you if you want."

I look at the waiter, who is smiling brightly. Everything about him is perfect from his teeth, nose, lips, jaw and even his hair. I stand abruptly and lean into him, inhaling as deeply as I can. "Nope, you don't smell like Roman."

"No, ma'am. I'm the vampire known as Gregory. I don't know Roman."

"Do you know all the vampires?"

He shakes his head. "There are many."

"But you're all related?"

"In a way, I suppose. Do you need me to call this Roman for you? Are you his consort?"

I'm sipping my drink when he says this, causing me to almost choke. "His what?"

"His mate or as some of the women here call it, his juice hustler."

My mouth drops open, and I snicker. "I'm not Roman's consort or a juice hustler."

"Okay, ma'am."

"Did you really say, juice hustler? What is that?"

"We call them donors, but some people like to mock us."

"I see."

"Ma'am, your machine is beeping. You need to play before it zeros out your funds, and you have to start all over."

Blindly I reach for the button and press it. I'm not done with this conversation, but also feel I shouldn't have it in the middle of a casino. I feel bad for asking Gregory all these questions, but now I'm curious. There are things I need to know. I pat the seat beside me, motioning for him to sit down.

"I really shouldn't."

"You should." I raise my eyebrow, fully expecting him to do as I've asked. After he looks around, he finally relents and takes the seat next to me. "I have questions. You will answer them, right?" I look deep into his eyes, waiting for an answer.

"A human cannot compel a vampire."

"I know."

"Please stop looking into my eyes, you're creeping me out."

I blanch at this statement. Shouldn't I be the one creeped out by him? He's dead for God sake. His heart doesn't beat... but everything else works! The words of Lana replay loudly in my mind. I find myself looking at his crotch while thinking about what she said.

"Are you the one who fucks Lana?" I ask, in my drunken stupor.

"I'm going to go get you some water and see if I can find this Roman you speak of." Before I can tell Gregory to stay, he's gone lightning fast. I have no choice but to leave. I don't want Roman showing up here nor do I want to see him. He needs to understand we can never, ever do business together and the sooner he figures this out, the better we'll all be.

9

ROMAN

*I*nitially, I had decided to give Fiona some space after our lunch. She is a complicated creature, and the last thing I want to do is overwhelm her. I need her to view me not as a monster, but as a man, who has desires and feelings, and I think she will start to see that after she reads my business plan. I've intentionally not shared my plans with my vampire brethren. Many wouldn't understand my desire to help humans in the way I want to, and it's none of their business. I've spent hundreds of years on this earth doing what I want, and it's time to give back. It's not a common emotion that vampires experience being an elite species. It's certainly not something I thought I'd want to do.

Now it's been two days, and she hasn't contacted me. I've thought of her nonstop, and as it turns out, vampires get anxiety, an emotion I don't recall experiencing. I'm nervous and agitated, finding myself running my hands through my hair, pacing incessantly. My need to act is overwhelming, so I decide to reach out to her. When she doesn't pick up the phone, I angrily press the end call button, not leaving a message. I miss the days when I could slam the phone receiver back into the cradle with frustration. Pressing the button on my smartphone isn't nearly as satisfying. Throughout the day, I try calling her several times, leaving no messages. I'm not sure what to say on her voicemail, and I want to hear her voice.

It occurs to me that she may be conflicted still. I'm quite certain that my plan to help children in Las Vegas appeals to her emotionally, but she could also be trying to figure out how to handle her father. She has a superficial exterior, but I know I've touched her in some way. How do I know? I couldn't begin to explain, but I know.

So, I rack my brain for a plan B. It's clear that I haven't impressed her quite enough to take the initiative in contacting me herself, or she's still scared. I surmise that more effort is the only way to get in her good graces, as I've given her plenty of time to mull it over on her own. A more aggressive approach is the next phase. I look for her, not so I can confront her directly, but so I can watch and learn more about her. What she likes. What she desires. Besides me. I know she desires me, but she isn't ready for that. It's not hard to find her, even in a city this size. A connection of some kind draws me to her, like an electromagnetic pull. It would trouble me if I didn't like it so much; seeing her is like getting a fix.

I find her at the mall, with her vampire friendly acquaintance, shopping. I've become quite the detective these days, on a stakeout more or less, just watching and listening to her. Her smile is like sunshine. It infects everyone who she comes in contact with, myself included. I watch her interact with salespeople, she's kind to everyone. She looks everyone in the eye, takes her time with her exchanges, and is thoughtful in her responses.

When her friend asks where the third amigo is, Fiona replies, a guilty tone in her voice. "I didn't ask Leslie to come."

"Why not?" Lana asks, seemingly shocked.

"Well, because I'm kind of tired of being lectured about the monster vampires, and I'm simply not up for it today."

"Ooh, did something happen with Roman?" She emphasizes my name.

"Not exactly." I watch her hesitate and think about her next words carefully. "I mean sort of. We had lunch together a couple of days ago, and we talked."

Giddy with excitement, Lana claps her hands together. "Did you fuck him?" Her enthusiasm for banging vampires is almost over the top, even for a vampire. I wonder if it is that big of a difference? I know that vampires are more viral, more alluring; we can go far longer than our mortal counterparts, but I'd never fucked a vampire before I was a vampire myself. Lana's excitement leads me to believe there is a significant difference, and my mind wanders to giving Fiona the pleasure that Lana is clearly experiencing.

Slapping her friend on the arm, Fiona lets out a stifled laugh. "No! We had lunch. And we talked. That's it. But..."

"But what? You want to bang him. That's obvious."

"I don't know about that. But, I learned some things that have made me think that maybe your way of... open-minded thinking is far more who I am. Certainly more so than what my parents taught me. I feel like I have been brainwashed by my dad, and I think Roman is a nice guy."

I give a small fist pump to the air hearing this. My plan seems to be working. What started as winning the bid, has turned into winning the girl.

"So, explain how you had lunch with a vampire. They

don't eat. And then tell me why he's a nice guy. And if that's the case, why are you not banging him yet?"

"Really Lana, you're nothing but a sex kitten these days aren't you?"

"Maybe, but this isn't about me. Spill!"

"Well, he's a gentleman first of all. He's done nothing but try to make me see that he's not some kind of monster, but it's more than that."

"Like what?"

"Well, he asked me to read his business proposal. So, I did. And you're never going to believe what he wants the casino for."

"I'm on the edge of my seat!"

"He wants to use it to fund a place that houses the homeless and helps foster kids. Like he wants to use the money to help humans."

"Get the hell out of here." Lana sounds shocked. Why they all think none of us give a fuck about their well being is beyond me. We all live in the same society for Christ's sake. It doesn't give me much joy to see homeless people, or to see children suffer, just because I can't have my own. Vampires have a soul. Folklore and propaganda have really fucked us over the years. It makes me sad to see anyone suffer; I hope that she sees this in me soon.

"I'm dead serious. He wants to use the money to help people. I wish I could help him, I really do. But my dad is never going to listen."

"Well, that may be the case now, but you don't know that it will always be that way." Lana sounds optimistic, which could be good.

"I don't think so. My dad would kill me himself if he knew that I had lunch with a vampire in the first place.

Anyway, he's tried calling me a few times, and I haven't taken his calls."

"Well, why the hell not?"

"Because I can't help him, and that's all he wants anyway." My jaw drops at her words.

Fuck. No. That's not all I want! I want to run over there and tell her that's not my only desire, but I know I can't give up my hiding spot. She'd probably be super pissed that I was stalking her on a regular basis, to begin with.

"What even makes you think that? From what you have said and hinted at, I think there's more to this little thing than you realize."

Yes! Listen to your friend, Fiona! She knows what she's talking about.

"Well, ultimately, I can't help him. I'm not going to call him back. It's nothing but asking for trouble. Even if he does seem like a great guy."

"I think you're cutting your nose off to spite your face. Frankly, you should give this a bit of a chance. It wouldn't kill you, pardon the pun, to get out with someone besides clients and me and Leslie. You haven't dated in forever, and I think - no, I know - you're missing out."

I like this Lana. I need to send her some flowers or something. She's a good friend, and smart. Fiona doesn't reply, and it looks like that is the end of the conversation for now. I decide to follow them around some more. It's time to step up my courtship game, high society style. While I'm mildly offended that Fiona thinks all I want is her dad's signature on my papers, I can also see why she might think that. I thought we had more of a connection at lunch though, and I'm hoping that what I've got planned now will, at the very least, show her that I'm a man of action.

I trail the ladies to the next store, observing their activities and purchases. Finding out what Fiona likes, what she doesn't like, what she wants, but thinks is too expensive or what she's not sure about. When they leave the first store, a jewelry store, I approach the young man at the counter and ask what the ladies were looking at.

"The ladies who just left?" He looks at me, confused.

"Yes. Well actually, just the blonde. With the stunning blue eyes."

He smiles at me and nods his head, waving me over to a display. He pulls out a tray with platinum necklaces on it.

"She was looking at this one." He points to a dainty chain from which a tiny Egyptian ankh dangles. He smirks as it hits me. He already knew.

"You're sure, this is the one she was looking at?" I stare at the tiny symbol, recalling history.

"I'm sure, sir." He has realized that the significance has dawned on me.

"I'll take it."

"Right away, sir." He walks off to wrap up my purchase.

The Egyptian ankh, also known as the key of life, has long been a vampiric symbol. It originated as a cross with a handle, or crux anksata in Latin. Its meaning is eternal life. The progeny of vampires are dated back as far as time from ancient Greece. However, the ankh was a symbol found in hieroglyphics representing our culture in ancient Egypt. That is not a well known, or common fact. She's been doing her research.

I take my purchase, and follow the ladies from store to store, making purchases that demonstrate my attention to detail, and how I desire for her to have the things that she wants. But this necklace, it is special. And she will have it.

10

FIONA

"So what are your plans for the rest of the day?" I ask Lana in between bites of my Cobb salad. We've spent the day shopping and dodging Leslie. It's not that I wanted to spend the day without her, it's that I wanted to spend the day without her and Lana arguing. From the moment I met up with Lana, it's been my intention to ask her more about her vampire boyfriend, but I have yet to broach the subject.

I don't want to look like I'm eager for information, but I want to be well-educated. It's not that I'm interested in Roman because I'm not. I'm curious about... well, all of it. Vampires are stronger than humans are, so how does that work when it comes to sex? And what about eating? If you're having sex with one, does that give them permission to bite you?

"Fiona?"

"FIONA!"

"What? I'm sorry," I say as I shake my head. My fork falls from my hand, and I try to catch it before it crashes into my bowl, but end up batting it toward Lana instead. "Sorry," I mutter, reaching across the table to pick up my utensil. Ever since I met Roman, I've done nothing but think about sex, and sex with him. This isn't normal for me, and he's to blame. He has me under some vampire spell or something, which I'd like to point out, is against the law.

Would Roman stoop so low as to compel me to do his bidding? Is that how compulsion works? It's the only explanation as to why I can't get him off my mind. Unfortunately, it's working on me, but he'd have to do this to my father as well and considering how my dad feels, he'd probably try to drive a stake through Roman's heart.

"What is going on?" Lana reaches across the table and holds my hand. "You've been... off all day. Did you and Shan hook up or something? Are you pregnant?"

"Lana!" I look around and make sure no one's paying attention to us. My dad's friends are everywhere, and the last thing I need is for rumors to start about me. "God no, I'm not pregnant," I say through clenched teeth.

"So what gives?" she asks, sitting back.

I shrug and motion for her to lean forward. "It's Roman."

"I knew you slept with him."

Shaking my head, I say, "I have not nor do I plan to, but I can't get him off my mind, and I want to know if you feel the same way about your friend at the gym."

"Do you think he's compelling you? Because that's a huge no-no. My friend says their rules are strict and their creator doesn't want to go through the mass exodus again."

"Mass exodus?"

Lana brushes me off and scoots her chair next to mine. "Tell me everything."

"There isn't anything to tell, Lana. I just feel... I don't know. I think about him all the time, and I don't know him.

When I close my eyes, he's there. He's in my dreams, and I feel like he's watching me all the time. He knows things too. Like where to find me."

"Enhanced hearing, plus he's probably bored during the day, so he's listening for you. My friend says we each have a distinct sound and once they hone in on it, they can pretty much follow our voices until they've found us. It's like GPS for vamps or something."

"So he can just show up whenever he wants?"

"Yes and no," Lana says, shrugging. "They have to be within a mile or so of the person they're looking for."

I sit back and sigh. "This is all so creepy. Do you know how crazy this is making me? Last night I went to a casino and tried to compel a vampire. Like, who does this? Me," I say, pointing to my chest. "Why did I have to meet him?"

Lana picks a piece of avocado out of her salad and drops it into her mouth. After she licks her fingers, she smiles. "You know everything happens for a reason."

"Maybe for Roman, but not for me. He sought me out because of who my father is, and now I can't get him off my mind."

"Is he hot?" My mouth drops open, and her smile widens. "Tell me!"

"Ugh, I don't want him to be, but Lana, he is. Everything about him seems perfect, and I know it's to entice humans, yet I can't stop thinking about his black hair and what it'd feel like to run my fingers through it, or to stare into his vibrant blue eyes. He's been made to be this good-looking man and deadly creature. It's a no-win situation."

Our waitress approaches our table asking if we need a refill on anything. When we tell her no, she leaves the bill on the table and tells us to take our time. I glance around my favorite restaurant, loving the outside seating with the ivy weaved throughout the pergola, offering the perfect amount of shade.

"Are you going to let your father dictate your life?"

"Not everyone is like your parents, Lana."

"You're right, I'm very lucky. However, you're an adult, with a college education. Just think, you could tell daddy dearest no and actually get a job and put your degree to use. You'd be able to move back to California."

"You'd miss me," I tease her. She's right though, Vegas is nothing more than a stop over for me. The only reason I'm here is because of my father, and truthfully, I'd really like to put my marketing degree to work.

Lana and I part ways on the Strip, kissing each other on the cheeks. When I asked her what she's going to do, she told me she has a date with her vampire. Of course, she winked and headed toward the gym she works out at. I was tempted to follow her so I could watch her interact with this man, but my mind isn't right, and I don't want to embarrass her.

Instead of taking a cab home, I decide to walk. The streets are ridiculously busy, and by the time I reach my hotel, I've been hit, jostled, and pushed by tourists rushing from casino to casino or trying to find a prime spot to watch the Bellagio fountains.

"Good evening, Ms. Weston," the bellhop says. I smile and thank him for holding the door that'll lead me to a private elevator, which goes directly to the penthouses. Waiting for the lift is my neighbor, who eyes me up and down. He's married, and here he is, trying to pick his tongue up off the ground. My stranger danger radar is going off, causing me to turn on my Jimmy Choo's and head back toward the door. "Everything okay, Ms. Weston?"

"Yes, I decided to run down to the little shop for a

snack." I'm not hungry, but I'm not getting into the elevator with my sleazy neighbor either. Lord knows what could happen. Down at the store, I grab some candy and a bottle of water. Two things I do not need but feel it'd be rude to not buy something. This is how I spent most of my day shopping with Lana. Touching things I want, but couldn't bring myself to buy for no rhyme or reason.

Walking through the casino is never my idea of a good time, but this is one of the rare hotels that actually has its elevators near the check-in, meaning travelers don't have to push their luggage through a carpeted space jam-packed with gamblers. I know, it's all a ploy to get the tourists to stop and put money down on the table, but there are people who would like to get to their room without breaking a sweat.

The public elevator is full of young drunk co-eds, having the time of their lives. This used to be me. My sorority sisters and I would pack up for the weekend and come over, staying in luxurious suites, partying it up all night and sleeping all day. Mondays used to be such a drag.

I'm the last one left as the lift heads to the top floor. After the day I've had, I can't wait to slip into something comfortable and crash out on my couch with some chick flick determined to remind me true love does exist.

As soon as I open my door, I know my plan for the night isn't going to happen. Immediately, I start to sneeze, and my eyes begin to water. The gladiolus, roses, snapdragons, and irises are all beautiful, but I'm allergic, and I have no idea how they ended up in my suite.

In a panic, I rush to my balcony to seek out some fresh air, tripping over a box on the floor. Holding my breath, I glance around and see every few feet there are black, blue and turquoise boxes all over my living room. I struggle to get the terrace door open, and once I do, I inhale dry air, which doesn't do much for me. Thankfully, I had the wherewithal to hold onto my purse and am able to find an allergy pill to swallow with my newly bought bottle of water. "What the hell?" I mutter as I dial the front desk.

"What can I do for you, Ms. Weston?"

"Come get these damn flowers out of my house. It says right there in my file that I'm allergic, so I want to know who opened my door so the damn florist could try and kill me!"

"Um..."

"Um isn't an answer. Come get these before I die." I hang up the phone and squeeze my legs together as I battle through another round of sneezing. My eyes are sealing shut, and my nose is running. "I can't believe someone would do this to me." I'm on the verge of tears and desperate to be able to breathe.

After ten minutes and no bellhop, I contemplate climbing over the edge of the balcony and Spidermaning my way down to the front desk, but death isn't high on my priority list right now. No, now I want to find and kill the person who did this to me.

"I give up." I pull my jacket over my face and blindly head toward my door, hitting my head when I don't stop in time. In the hall, the air is somewhat better, but not enough to stop the reaction. Inside the elevator, my reflection scares me. My face is red, eyes are puffy, and my nose is enlarged from the constant rubbing I'm doing. "I don't know who hates me so much to do this!" I cry out, adding more insult to injury.

When I reach the bottom floor, I stalk toward the concierge, pointing to my face. "This! Do you see this face? What does it say when you pull up my suite? I'm pretty sure it's in bold letters that Ms. Weston is allergic to flowers, and only plants should be allowed upstairs. So tell me why my apartment is full of flowers that make me look like this?"

"Ahem."

I turn at the sound of a throat clearing to find Roman, the stalker vampire standing behind me with a bouquet of roses in his hands. They're red and beautiful, and part of me wants to take them from him, but the other part, the angry part, steps forward and looks at him through my squinted watery eyes and reaches for the flowers. Roman hands them over with a smile.

"I hate you!" I say as I bash him over the head repeatedly with the flowers. "Do you have any idea what you've done to me?"

In his defense, he stands there and takes the beating, never flinching. Somewhere behind me, the staff is chuckling, and they're lucky there aren't more flowers at my quick disposal because I'd beat them as well.

11

ROMAN

*A*s I wait in the lobby, I can't help but be pleased with myself. I've not only showered her with gifts, but I've also paid attention. All the things I'm certain she likes. Suddenly, a blonde tornado flies out of the elevator yelling and throwing her hands in the air violently. When she catches my attention, she rushes at me like a Viking shield maiden. Her long locks swing violently behind her as she approaches, and when she grabs the flowers from my hand, I realize she is not happy, at all.

As she batters me with the roses, I take the hits, completely unsure of what they're for. When the area is sufficiently strewn with rose petals, and she's no longer thrashing the stems at me, she stops, huffing and wheezing before me.

"Why would you do this to me?" she demands as tears and snot run down her face.

"I thought it would make you happy," I reply calmly, grabbing a handkerchief from my pocket. A habit I picked up many years ago, I almost always had one with me, even though I rarely needed it.

She slams the tattered stems on a nearby counter and takes the handkerchief from me, wiping her eyes and nose. "You thought poisoning me was something I would like? What the hell is wrong with you, Roman?"

Realizing now my research wasn't nearly as thorough as I'd thought, I make a note to think about human ailments in the future. Who would have thought that a room full of beautiful flowers would do this to her? Certainly not me. "Fiona, I'm so sorry. Let me make it up to you," I plead, attempting to take her hand.

She snatches her hand back quickly. "I think I've had just about enough of you." She turns to the nearby staff, all staring at her now. "Please send someone up to remove the flowers from my suite. Send them over to the church on Second Avenue."

"I had no idea they would have this... effect on you. I am truly sorry that my gesture took a turn. Please, let me do something." I do feel like an ass now, and I'm really not sure how to fix this other than to take her someplace where there are no flowers so she can recover from the episode. Allergies aren't something I've ever dealt with in my lifetime; I can't recall a time where a woman didn't adore receiving them.

"Roman." She sneezes into my handkerchief. "Roman, I don't know what your game is, but I'm not playing. I already told you that I can't help you. My father isn't going to sign your papers. So, buying me a bunch of gifts, even if the flowers I am deathly allergic to were well-meaning, doesn't change anything. I think you should just go."

The thing is, her tone doesn't suggest I should go. Her puffy swollen eyes, now bluer than the Greek Isles, are saying something completely different. They're asking me to give her a reason I should stay. I fondle the jewelry box in my pocket that contains the ankh necklace I purchased earlier. It's clear that now isn't the right time to give it to her. That one I'll wait on. It deserves the perfect moment, and this surely isn't it.

"Fiona, let's get some fresh air. You can't go to your apartment while they're cleaning it out, so how about a walk?"

She gives me an apprehensive look, but finally nods and walks with me silently. Once we get outside into the fresh air, she takes a deep breath. She appears to be less affected by the allergens now, but before I have the opportunity to apologize again, she begins.

"What were you thinking, Roman? Honestly? What's with all the stuff? I don't need any of it, and getting me things isn't going to change the fact that I can't help you." She appears exasperated and heaves out a breath.

"Honestly, I was just trying to win your affections."

"Win my affections? What on earth for?"

"Because I like you, Fiona. Isn't it obvious?"

"What's obvious, is that you did your research about me. Not enough obviously, or you wouldn't have tried to kill me today. I may seem like some high society idiot, but I'm not! You can't buy me, Roman, and you better not compel me either." Her face is serious, which troubles me.

I stop her, grabbing her arm and looking at her directly, so I'm sure I have her full attention. "Listen to me, Fiona," I say sternly. "I did not try to kill you. In the beginning, yes, I was trying to get your help, and I may have resorted to looking into you a bit, but that isn't why I sent you the gifts." Crossing her arms and meeting my stare, she watches as my lips move.

"Why did you get me all those gifts?"

"As a sign of affection," I admit. In retrospect, I can see that it was too much.

"Affection?"

"You said yourself that you're not a stupid woman. Can you not tell when a man is interested in you?" I ask, a smirk forming.

As she squints at me, I can see her lips beginning to form what looks like a smile. "This doesn't make any sense, Roman."

"Why not? Because you wear a cross? All that means is that I'm not to compel you, and I respect your decision. However, it doesn't mean I cannot desire you. It just means it has to be your choice. I've never tried to be anything I'm not with you. I would like for you to see the real me, Fiona."

Her hand raises to the cross she wears, and as she gently fondles it, I hope that she's thinking about what I've said as her face flushes. I can hear her heartbeat picking up, and before she has a chance to run away, I decide to change the subject and show her I'm more than the research she has done on vampires. Just like she has shown me.

"Come, I'd like to show you something."

"You're not going to take me back to your lair are you?" she asks.

"Not today. I have something else I'd like to show you," I reply, ignoring her sarcasm completely.

I hail us a cab and open the door for her to climb in the back before me. I can't help but notice her perfect ass in front of me and fuck if I don't want to take her back to my lair, as she calls it. A penthouse apartment of my own actually, but she can call it whatever the fuck she wants. I give the driver an address, as we take off toward the south end of the Strip.

"Where are we going?" she asks softly.

"I know you read my proposal, and I'd like to show you something."

"Roman, I already told you that I can't help –"

I interrupt her. "I'm not taking you there because I think you can help me. I'm taking you there, so you'll begin to understand that I'm a man with more to him than fangs. I have a heart. I am capable of empathy, of philanthropy... of love." That last one leaves me trailing from my own sermon. I don't love her, not yet, but something about her makes me think I could. That I will. It's not something I can describe in particular detail; however, I'm certain she needs to see me as more than the folklore she's been brainwashed to believe. She needs to see the real me.

As we pull up to the brick building, I pay the driver and get out of the taxi, holding my hand for Fiona. To my surprise, and my pleasure, she takes it as she slides out onto the street, staring at the building before us.

"Is this the foster home that you're trying to fund?" she asks, still holding my hand.

"It is. It's actually sort of a halfway house for wayward foster children who haven't found a good home or are difficult to place. Come on, I'll show you around." I pull at her hand, and she comes with me seeming to inspect the area.

I am currently supplementing the funding of the home and covering the costs that taxpayer dollars do not take care of, along with some additional funds for improvements and activities for the kids. It needs more work, and with my plan and the casino funding, this home would work like a well funded private school and sanctuary for the kids.

"How is this paid for now? With tax dollars?" she asks, taking her hand back, and running it along the worn bricks outside.

"Yes, and some private funding."

Just then, the door opens and Mrs. Connolly, the headmistress of sorts, comes out to greet me.

"Roman! It's wonderful to see you!" She gives me a huge hug, her round frame enveloping me. "I see you've brought a friend." She winks at me.

"Mrs. Connolly, this is Fiona Weston. I wanted to show her the place. I've been telling her about our plans."

"Oh Fiona, it's lovely to meet you. Our Roman has just been so wonderful. The kids absolutely adore him. Did you know that he was a soccer player? They actually started a little regular game since he taught them all how to play." She swoops Fiona into a hug, much to her surprise, which makes me chuckle.

"It's very nice to meet you too, Mrs. Connolly." Fiona's caught off guard by Mrs. Connolly's immediate affection but seems to soften more and more.

"It's arts and crafts time right now if you'd like to come in and see what everyone is working on?"

"That would be lovely," Fiona replies. Her interest gives me a chill, or butterflies I suppose. Whatever it is, it's feelings, towards her, and they continue to grow with each moment I spend with her.

Mrs. Connolly leads us inside where the children are all sitting at easels, painting. "Everyone! Mr. Roman is here! Let's say hello to him and his friend, Miss Fiona."

As the class all say hello to us in unison, a huge smile forms on Fiona's face, and she leans into me. This is the exact reaction I was hoping for. Perhaps the flowers and gifts were too far over the top, and I needed the reminder of our humanity outside of superficial tokens myself.

After we spend some time talking with Mrs. Connolly and getting a very enthusiastic tour from a few of the kids, I promise I'll be back tomorrow for soccer practice, and we bid them farewell. Out on the front curb, as we wait for the ride I called, Fiona sighs quietly.

"What's wrong?" I ask.

"Nothing at all. Thank you for bringing me here." She smiles up at me.

"You're welcome. They're wonderful, aren't they?" It feels good to share something special with her.

"How does the casino help your cause more than providing the donation you give currently?"

"Well, the idea is that the casino already funds public education as part of the Nevada tax laws, but as a private owner, I can also make a deal with the government to fund their home locally. Also, I'm planning to initiate a work-study program that will allow for the kids who haven't found jobs and who are old enough to work, guaranteed employment at the casino. Any student who works at the casino will have their income matched directly with cash that goes into a college fund to support their higher education. This means that they continue to support the community, and round and round it goes. It will sustain itself long term by continuing to give back over and over."

"That's genius, Roman." She smiles.

"It gets better. I'm sure you read this in my proposal, but another portion of the plan is to train and employ homeless in the city, and in return, I will use net profits from the casino to house them as well. In a similar halfway house environment, which will allow them to save the money they make so they can get on their own feet again."

"So, you won't be making any actual profit on the casino?" she asks.

"No. I don't need money. I need to help people, Fiona. That's what I've been trying to show you."

"So you have," she replies thoughtfully as our ride pulls up.

12

FIONA

*R*oman opens the door of the cab for me. His hand glides along the small of my back as I slide in. These subtle touches aren't lost on me. I noticed he wasn't in any hurry to let go of my hand when we arrived at the orphanage, nor has he stopped trying to touch me since. I should complain. I should be pissed because he hasn't listened to a word I've said, but I'm not. I'm in complete awe by how much of a gentleman he is. Shan would never open the door for me, unless other high society folks were around, let alone touch me in the most sensual, yet common way possible. It's like Roman knows women, and while he may be a vampire, something tells me his overall experience is minimal.

I glance at him, only to find him staring at me. The fact a vampire is watching me should creep me out, but it doesn't. I match his gaze, waiting to see who will crack and smile first. I win when his pearly whites start to show through his parted lips. "I win," I tell him, winking.

"I wasn't aware we were in some sort of competition."

"A stare off."

Roman chuckles. "Surely, if I had known, I would've won."

"Which is exactly why I didn't say anything. Sometimes a woman needs to win."

"And what did you win?" Roman moves closer. His hand is dangerously close to mine. It would be so easy to slide the few inches along the leather seat until my hand is touching his. Everything in me is screaming to pull away, to give him the cold shoulder, but I don't. This time, I make a move. It's bold and unlike me, but I felt something earlier when he was holding my hand. His colder than normal skin didn't bother me as much as I thought it would.

"This," I say as I slip my hand into his, interlocking our fingers together. Roman's smile grows wider, and I find myself looking for his fangs, waiting for them to drop down and for him to attack me. The driver of this cab wouldn't do anything, I'm sure, but deep down I know Roman isn't going to hurt me.

"I like this," he says, his eyes never leaving mine as he brings our conjoined hands to his lips. They linger there for a moment before he pulls away. The kiss sends shivers down my spine. Not because the man holding my hand to his mouth is a natural born killer, but because this is literally the most sensual act I have ever had bestowed upon me.

How can this be possible? I dated Shan off and on for years. Was he not sensual? Did he not care about me? I'm sure in his own way he did. We were good together, dubbed the up and coming power couple until I chose to pursue a life in California.

"I do too." My voice is soft, and the words are out of my mouth before I realize what I'm saying. I expect Roman to grin like the Cheshire cat, but he doesn't. He smiles softly and continues to hold our hands on his lap.

"I'm sorry about earlier, with the flowers. Had I known..."

"It's fine. It's one the reason I've stayed in Nevada for so long. The desert helps keep my allergies at bay. Everything is--"

"Dead?" he interrupts. It would be easy to say he's putting words in my mouth, but this isn't the case.

"But you're not dead, are you?"

Roman's eyes tear away from mine, in time for the cab driver to pull over in front of the hotel where I live. Roman pays and exits the cab first, never letting go of my hand. Not all I have learned about vampires seems to hold true when it comes to Roman. He's soft, gentle and doesn't move lightning fast, although I'm sure when he's with his own kind things are different. He hasn't tried to coerce me into anything, at least nothing I'm aware of. I can easily say these feelings are genuine because as I stand here on the street corner, watching this creature survey the crowd like we're finishing our first date and both wondering if the awkward kiss should happen here or at the elevator, I realize I don't want my day with him to end. I like holding his hand, and I like being in his presence, but loathe the idea that we've come together because of business. Why couldn't I meet him on my own?

"Would you like me to check and see if your apartment has been cleared out?"

"It's nice of you to ask but no. Would you like to get dinner at the Bellagio?" I point behind me, the nerves of the moment setting in. "I mean, I know you don't eat, but it's a vampire-friendly restaurant and maybe..."

"If you're thinking I drink blood while dining, the answer is no." Roman steps forward and his free hand reaches toward my face. I too take a step closer, expecting him to cup my cheek, but he moves my hair away from my neck and uses humanly impossible strength to tilt my head to the side. Roman presses himself to me and my heartbeat increases. I seek out help from any of the passersby, but they're oblivious or so used to see something like this, they don't care to ask if I need help. "This is how I feed." His nail trails down my throat, and I swallow hard. "But only if you allow me," he whispers into my ear.

Roman steps away, his expression solemn. "I will never take unless you offer, Fiona."

"And if I never offer?"

He frowns and shakes his head. "A conversation for another place?"

I nod, understanding that his situation is private, and not all humans are privy to what a vampire does when it doesn't concern them. "Dinner?"

Roman tightens his grip on my hand and leads us toward the crosswalk. I find myself leaning into him when other women look him up and down. All vampires are devil-ishly handsome. It's the appeal they're reborn with to lure humans to them, but Roman is different. The always there stubble is a definite turn on and his eyes... they're so blue and translucent, I feel like I could see into the depths of his soul if he had one. Of course, I'm saying this without really knowing him. It's my gut telling me otherwise, and my father has always told me to follow my instincts.

Even though I invited Roman out to dinner, he's taken control, powering us through the onslaught of tourists and into the hotel with a commanding air about him. I suppose from the outside we could look like any other power couple in Vegas, and it's only his paler than normal skin that gives him away because his mark is covered by the way we're walking side by side.

We arrive at the restaurant and stand at the podium, waiting for the hostess. By the number of people waiting, it'll be an hour wait, easily.

"Roman!" I look for the source of his name and find one of the waitresses rushing toward us. Well, not us, but Roman. I fully expect him to drop my hand to greet the woman, but he doesn't. He holds on tighter. Shan would've let go.

"Lydia, how are you?" Roman kisses her on the cheek. He lets go of my hand, but only so he can place his arm behind my back to pull me forward. "This is my Fiona," Roman tells her. The fact he calls me "his" sends another shiver down my spine. I love it.

"So nice to meet you, Fiona. Are you here for dinner?"

I nod. "We were about to put our names on the list."

Lydia waves us off. "No need. Follow me; I just had a table open in my station."

Roman doesn't hesitate to fall in line behind her. Me, my radar is going off, and my jealousy meter is starting to spike. How do they know each other? Were they intimate? Did he bite her?

Lydia smiles softly as she shows us to our table for two, overlooking the fountains. I don't care how many times I've taken in the views of Las Vegas, the Strip, once the sun starts going down is a sight to behold. Roman holds out my chair and orders a red wine for me to drink. As soon as she's gone, I ask him, "Is she a juice hustler of yours?"

Roman's eyes go wide. He looks over his shoulder, possibly checking to see if Lydia heard me or maybe he's seeking out other vampires, hoping they didn't hear what I said. Ah hell, I don't know. Roman stands and pulls his chair over to mine, resting his arm on the back of my chair. I like this. It feels intimate. He reaches for my hand and holds it in my lap. "Absolutely not. Lydia's married to my friend, who is a vampire," he says quietly.

"Oh."

"If you have questions, I will answer them, Fiona. I meant what I said earlier, I like you, and while my intentions at first were business related, that was all before I had a chance to get to know you. You're an amazing woman." He brushes my hair behind my ear. I turn and look at him.

"Do you have a juice hustler? Someone who lives in your lair that services you?"

Roman smirks and shakes his head. "No, I don't. When I need to feed, I go to our club."

"And you have sex with them?"

He shakes his head again. "Feeding and sex don't go hand in hand. I can bite someone anywhere to feed off them." Roman nuzzles my neck as his lips dance along my skin, undoubtedly feeling my pulse vibrate. "But here..." His nose runs a path down my neck. "I'll bite here when the time is right. When I sense you're close, and you need the extra endorphins to push you over the edge, or when I want to make love to you, I'll nip ever so lightly so you can feel my hunger for you. And sometimes, it's just fun to play."

"Does it hurt?"

"It can, if you're rough with your subject, but Fiona, I can promise you, I'd never do anything to hurt you."

"How can I be so sure?"

Roman adjusts, which I find odd considering he could literally stand for days and never move or flinch. Many vampires work as window models because of their ability to be statues for long periods of time, not to mention their good looks. But Roman, without knowing his age, it makes me wonder if he's worked hard to blend in or if he's really kept his humanity over the years.

"Honestly, you can't be sure. Just as you can't be sure if a human wouldn't hurt you. Life is a gamble, Fiona, but I'm an honest man."

"My friend says you're not a man, but a monster. An abomination."

"Created by gods," he says as he looks away. I feel as if he's growing uncomfortable. Instead, he turns and looks into my eyes. "Everyone is entitled to his or her opinion. I'm asking you to form your own by getting to know me. Spend time with me, Fiona. Learn about who I am and decide for yourself."

"Okay, but can you do me a favor?"

"Name it." Roman smiles.

"Kiss me."

"With pleasure," he says seconds before his lips press against mine, and his hands gently cup my face. Anyone who says vampires are made of concrete is wrong. Roman's lips are soft and move fluidly against mine. He parts my lips easily and slides his tongue into my mouth, causing me to moan. His taste is intoxicating, and I need more.

"Don't."

"What?"

"Moan," he says. "I may be a vampire, but my human parts still work the same and feeling you moan does things to me that shouldn't happen in restaurants."

I think about laughing, but the idea quickly goes away when he returns to kissing me. This time he doesn't hesitate to deepen the kiss, and I don't hold back either, that is until my tongue drags across one of his fangs.

13

ROMAN

I'm completely fucked. Her kiss is sweeter than anything I've tasted in my lifetime. She runs her delicious tongue along my teeth, and comes upon a fang, stopping suddenly and pulling away. She raises her small hand to her lips while examining me.

"Oh!" she exclaims softly, looking surprised, or perhaps even confused.

"What's wrong?" I ask, hoping the moment hasn't passed.

"I just.. I didn't realize..."

"That I had fangs?" I interject with a slight grin. It's the elephant in the room it seems, so I figure let's cut to the chase.

"Well, no. I mean, I knew you did. I was just surprised to feel them." She lowers her eyes to her lap where she's placed both her hands.

Gently, I rest one hand on hers, and with the other, I lift her chin, so she meets my eyes. "Fiona," I pause, looking for the right words. "I know that this is new, and perhaps even strange in some ways. Let's have some dinner, and some polite conversation to go with it, and you may ask me anything you're even remotely curious about. How does that sound?"

I watch as a sweet, almost bashful smile forms. "I would like that, Roman." She turns her hands over, so she's holding mine softly and says, "Thank you for being so patient with me. It's just all such... undiscovered and new territory for me."

Now, I feel a grin of my own spread across my face. "There's no place that I would rather be than right here and now with you Fiona." She could explore this territory for the next thousand years as far as I'm concerned.

Lydia walks back to our table, smiling as always. Even though it's perfectly normal that she is married to a friend of mine, what's not normal is that he will outlive her by hundreds of years. "Roman, Fiona, are you ready to place your order?" She looks to Fiona first.

"Oh, I will have the filet. Rare please." I can't help but find this choice funny, and I let out a bit of a chuckle.

"What?" Fiona asks, looking confused and furrowing her eyebrows at me.

Before I can answer that I'm amused by her choice in raw meat for dinner, Lydia steps in to stop me from acting a fool.

"Honey, he doesn't even eat. Ignore him. You gotta get some food in your system to keep up with them, believe me." She winks at Fiona and flashes her giant engagement ring and wedding band at her.

"Oh my God, is that a real blue diamond?" Fiona gasps, taking Lydia's hand for a moment, staring at it sparkle.

"It sure is. When your honey has been investing since

investing was invented, you end up with nice things. I'm a damn lucky girl in this lifetime. He had it mined just for me at the Cullinan Diamond Mine in South Africa. I still can't believe it. My Damen takes wonderful care of me, spoils me rotten. Now can I get you anything else, honey?"

Fiona leans back smiling, and replies, "No, thank you."

"And for you, honey?" Lydia turns to me.

"Nothing for me," Roman says, which I know Lydia already expected.

"Okay, you two. I'll be back soon to check on you." She walks off.

"Is everything ok?" I notice Fiona is looking around the room, assessing people at every table.

"Oh, shit. Yes, I'm sorry. I was just looking around, I've never eaten here before myself. And I typically don't go to very many... vampire friendly restaurants."

"It's okay. You have a learning curve. I know this. You have questions; why don't you ask me?" I want her to be comfortable. My desire for her understanding of me, of my culture, is overwhelmingly important to me.

"Okay, well, first of all. It seems like it's perfectly normal for vampires and humans to go out to eat together, but only one of them is eating. I don't want to be rude and eat in front of you, and it feels strange to be the only one eating at the table. Is this weird for you?"

I smile at her question. Her concern with seeming insulting or impolite is adorable. "Well Fiona, I don't eat. So it would be silly for me to order food that would only go to waste. Unless of course, you want more food, in which case, I'd just order whatever you wanted. It's not at all rude though to answer your question."

"Okay, so where do you go to... eat? Drink? What do

you call it?" She bites her lower lip thoughtfully, distracting me with her sensual allure. She clearly has no clue how enticing she is, but I shake the thoughts free so I can answer.

"Typically, if I need to announce it, I would say that I need to eat. Just like you would. But among other vampires, I might say that I need to feed." I watch as she listens intently, seemingly without any judgment, absorbing what I'm saying, so I continue. "As for where I go to eat, generally, I go to Clutch. It is a bar owned by a vampire friend of mine that services the needs of vampires and their consorts. Vampires without a consort are able to find and meet, or meet up with humans who volunteer or desire to... assist in meeting our needs."

Fiona leans back, crossing her arms and pursing her lips. I've said something that troubles her. "And you expect me to believe that's not sexual?" I can sense that there's a twinge of jealousy, and I find it incredibly arousing.

The tease in me wants to draw attention to it, but I want her to continue asking me what she's curious about, so I refrain from joking with her about it just yet and reply honestly. "As I mentioned before, it's not always sexual. It can be if everyone involved wants it to be. But it's a need that we have to sustain life, just as you have the need for food to fuel your body as well."

"Hmm, interesting," she replies thoughtfully. Seemingly satisfied with the answer, she moves on. "What about sleep? I read that you don't need to sleep. Is that true?"

"That is true."

"So what do you do when everyone is sleeping?"

"I read. I talk to others. And I do live in a city that is alive all night long."

"Good point. Is that why you picked Las Vegas?"

"I picked Las Vegas because it meets my needs. It is a

vampire-friendly city, which is my preference of course. The discourse that still exists between humans and vampires will always exist in some ways I'm sure, just as there is discourse among different humans. But, this city offers me many opportunities to come and go as I please, and the multitude of interesting business propositions that it offers keeps me busy and intrigued."

"How old are you?" she asks.

"I am five hundred and thirty-two."

I cannot help but chuckle at how her jaw falls open. I find that every new expression she reveals endears me even further.

"Get out. You're old," Fiona teases me.

"Too old for you?" I shamelessly flirt now. I simply can't help it. All I want to do is leave this restaurant and take her back to my place. I don't even need to ravage her, even though it's been on my mind. I just don't want to share her right now, I'd like her all to myself.

Blushing, she gives me a coy smile. "I think you just make the cut. But it was close. If you were six hundred, I'd be out of here." She giggles, and the sound would make my heart thump against my chest if that were still possible.

I can sense she's becoming more accustomed to our differences, and words escape how thrilled I am to see it. Unable to help myself, I pull her to me for another kiss. As she softens into me, allowing me once again to taste how sweet she is, my thirst for her grows. I do want to bite her, and as I pull her to me, my thumb gently runs over her pulsating jugular, increasing my lust tenfold. Knowing that I can't, at least not yet, I wrap my hand around the nape of her neck into her hair, tugging just slightly, causing her to moan yet again.

I separate us by just an inch and lean toward her ear. I

can hear her heart beating rapidly; dramatically almost like a bass drum in my ears. "I told you not to moan like that in public. You don't understand what you do to me, Fiona," I whisper hoarsely, my throat feeling dry from greedy hunger.

Her hand begins to run along my thigh, toward my increasing hardness, and just at the moment when I think I'm going to lose my composure in public, someone lets out a stifled cough at our table. It's Lydia, with Fiona's raw steak.

"Sorry to interrupt you two, but your dinner is ready, honey." She grins, setting the bloody steak in front of Fiona.

Slightly flustered, and righting herself, Fiona replies, "Oh, I um.. Thank you so much." Her face turns red, and she tries to smile.

"No problem. I'll leave you two alone. Just holler if you need me."

Turning to me, Fiona says in a hushed tone, "Oh my God, that's so embarrassing."

Generally speaking, vampires don't get embarrassed. We honestly don't give a fuck what other people think when it comes to such things. "You shouldn't be embarrassed, Fiona. You're a beautiful woman. Every man here wishes he were me right now." I watch her take in the words I've said, and while she may not believe me yet, I can see that she's letting her walls down with me. "Now eat. So I can walk you home and kiss you goodnight properly."

We lighten the conversation as I encourage her to feed herself. I can see that she still feels awkward being the only one at the table eating, and truthfully, I'd make myself eat if I could without getting sick just to make her happy. She's been looking around watching others most of the time we've sat here. While my organs are more or less the same as a human's, after all, I was human at one time, they don't process anything but blood now, and putting human food into my body would cause me physical sickness. It wouldn't kill me or anything dramatic like that, but since I don't have the enzymes to break down food or any of the chemistry for digestion, it has nowhere to go. I'll explain that to her eventually, but it doesn't feel like casual dinner conversation, particularly when I want her to hurry up and eat so I can kiss her again.

Once she's convinced me that she's had enough food, I pay the bill so we can go. It's getting late, and while I don't need sleep, I can see that she is tired. It's been a long day. "Thank you for dinner, Roman. You know you don't have to walk me all the way back to my place if it's out of the way," she says as I take her hand on our way out of the Bellagio.

"Under my watch, you get walked to your front door," I reply, squeezing her hand.

"And then?" she asks, a coy tone in her voice.

"Tonight?" I briefly contemplate what she's implying.

"Yes, tonight. You'll walk me to my door. And then..." She waits for me to pick up what she's put down on a seemingly silver platter.

Of course, I want to say, and then I take you inside and show you what it feels like to make love to a man who has the animal desire of the immortal. I want to tell her that inviting me to taste her blood would give us both more pleasure than she could imagine she is capable of, that it would connect us on an indescribable transcendental level. That exploring her body, one inch at a time, gently scraping my fangs along her curves would be my ultimate fantasy unleashed, and that providing her with intimate pleasure all night would be my greatest achievement.

What I actually say is, "And then I kiss you goodnight."

Every fiber of my being wants to move faster, wants to go all in. But I know it's too soon. She thinks she's ready, but she's not. I need to show her more before I can let her in completely.

14

FIONA

*I*t's been a few days since I decided to give Roman a chance, yet I've kept this to myself as if it's some dirty little secret. Lana won't care, but Leslie, she'd have an issue with what I'm doing, and frankly, I'm not ready to lose her friendship over a guy, human or vampire. Moreover, Leslie would say something to her parents, who would say something to my dad, and I don't want to deal with him right now. I already know how he feels, and I don't need him putting thoughts in my mind about Roman. I'm trying to give him a chance and keep an open mind. Broadcasting my personal life just invites unwanted advice.

With Roman, I'm having fun. Silly, stupid fun, but nonetheless each time I leave him at my door, breathless and wanting more from him, I'm grinning from ear to ear and squealing like a schoolgirl because he makes me happy. I can't recall a time when I've ever been romanced like this. After Roman's first mishap with flowers, which granted, he had no idea I was allergic to, and with the overly expensive jewelry, which he insisted I keep, Roman has been very tame with his gifts. I told him, little things go a long way. So, when he shows up with a pint of ice cream that hasn't melted because of his ice cold body temp, I can't help but fall for him a little bit more.

I stare at my reflection in the mirror, angling my head to the left and then to the right, elongating my neck. My fingers touch the spot where I think Roman would bite me if I were to allow. I know he wants to. He spends a long time touching the spot where my jugular is, and there have been brief moments when I've almost given in, but I can't bring myself to say those words. For one, pain. I'm weak and cry when I have a paper cut. The thought of his razor-sharp teeth breaking through my skin makes my stomach burn with fear. I know he said he'd never hurt me but come on, teeth ripping through flesh is going to hurt. Second, I hate the sight of blood. Third... well, I still have a problem accepting he's a vampire because he doesn't act like one. I don't know how many hours Roman has spent mimicking humans, but he's damn good at it, and honestly part of me wants to see his vampire side. The other part of me is like nope, the big bad vamp needs to stay hidden.

Still hanging from my neck is my cross. I don't know whether to take it off or not. Roman hasn't asked, not that I think he would, but I haven't asked him whether it makes him uncomfortable. I know it's supposed to relay the message I don't want to be compelled. However, some of my readings indicated that a cross could physically hurt a vampire. Is it painful for Roman to be with me? He hasn't said anything, not that I think he would, but still, the last thing I want is to cause him any unneeded pain.

My readings also say if a vampire doesn't eat, they'll experience discomfort, and that feeding is usually tied to a sexual encounter. I asked Roman if feeding is sexual and he says no, but Lana says otherwise. She's never given me a reason to doubt her, and as far as I'm concerned, she's my vampire expert. I could ask Lydia, but I don't know her well enough, and she's the wife of Roman's friend. Surely, they talk, and the last thing I want is for Roman to think I don't trust him. I do, but not fully.

The house phone rings and I rush from the bathroom to answer. "Hello."

"Ms. Weston, there's a Mr. Roman requesting access to your floor."

"Please send him up." Even though Roman knows he can come up anytime he wants, he's a gentleman and likes to announce his arrival. Truth be told, I like it, and I find myself pacing in front of my door, waiting for the elevator to ding. Once it does, my hand is resting on the knob, antici-pating his knock. I haven't seen Roman in ten hours, and as much as I want to think he's watching me while I sleep, I know he isn't. What he's doing though, I'd like to know. Meeting with other vampires doesn't exactly tell me much.

Roman's knock is soft considering he could easily tear my door off the hinges. I open it, with a smile on my face, and take in the man I'm enjoying spending all my free time with. He's standing there, with his hands in his pockets, looking as dashing as ever with his permanent stubble and icy blue eyes.

"Hi." One would think I've run a marathon by the way I sound right now. Somehow, running from the bathroom to the living room doesn't count as physical exercise.

"You look beautiful."

I look down at what I'm wearing. Chino shorts, black strappy sandals and a black tank top that doesn't scream stylish, but our plans for the day consist of taking a trip to Hoover Dam.

"I look plain and ordinary."

"There's nothing ordinary about you, Fiona." Roman's arm extends over the threshold, and his hand gently cups my face while his thumb brushes over my cheekbone. I turn and place a kiss on his palm. "We should go," he says, abruptly. "Are you wearing sunblock?"

"Yes, are you?" I counter, only to realize what I've said.

Roman laughs. "The sun doesn't bother me, make me sparkle or turn my body to dust. But you, on the other hand, could turn into what you humans refer to as a lobster, and from what I understand, you wouldn't want to be touched, and I can't have that, now can I?"

My insides alight with desire at his words. I swallow hard, trying to clear the lump that's formed in my throat. "No, I suppose we can't." I grab my purse and follow Roman to the elevator. We stand side by side until we've reached the bottom floor. He places his hand on my back to guide me out of the elevator and hotel where the valet is.

"We're this way." Roman directs me toward a cherry red Jeep Wrangler. The top is down and sitting in the back are Lydia and Damen. "You remember Lydia?"

"Yes, hi again," I say, accepting Roman's help as I climb in. Damen thrusts his hand forward, taking mine in his.

"I'm Damen, Lydia's husband."

"Hi, I'm--"

"Roman's," Damen says matter-of-factly. I glance at Roman, who's frowning.

"I brought you a hat," Roman says, handing me a baseball cap. "You might want it when we're on the freeway for the wind."

"Thank you." Within seconds, we're in the middle of the Las Vegas traffic heading toward Boulder City. The sun is hotter than I expected. Usually, I'm in the comfort of air conditioning, but I imagine being a vampire, feeling something like the wind in your hair and not having to worry about sunblock is nice.

As soon we're on the freeway, Roman's hand touches my leg. Instantly, my scorched skin cools down, and I realize why we're in a convertible. The hotter I am, the more I'll need Roman. It's a different form of chivalry, and I love it.

The drive is about forty minutes or so depending on traffic. We arrive the second the park opens, beating the crowd. After we park on the top floor of the parking structure, Roman and Damen lead Lydia and me to the stairs. "Hop on," Roman says, motioning to his back.

"Excuse me, what?"

Roman points to Lydia, who is about to get a piggyback ride from Damen.

"It'll be faster." He must sense my hesitation. I honestly can't remember the last time I've had a one of these. "I'll be safe."

"You're going to carry me down the stairs? I have two legs, I can walk perfectly fine."

"No one's saying you can't walk. But if I carry you, we get down to the bottom faster."

"Why didn't you just park down there?" I ask, jutting my foot out.

For the first time since I've met him, Roman rolls his eyes. "Because sometimes vampires are over the top and we like to use the abilities we have for fun. We happen to love racing downstairs."

I look to Lydia for confirmation. "It's true. We live on the top floor of our apartment complex and have yet to use the elevator."

"Not true," Damen says. "We used it for sex."

Lydia swats Damen on the shoulder. "We broke the

elevator and have been afraid to use it ever since." Damen laughs and shrugs.

"You won't drop me?"

"Never, Fiona." Roman helps me onto his back and makes sure I'm secure. "You may want to close your eyes." I do as he says, shutting my eyes and wrapping my arms around his neck. I suppose if I hang on too tightly, he won't choke to death.

No sooner do I close my eyes, Roman taps my leg, signaling for me to get down. I open my eyes slowly and look around. A few people are staring, probably wondering why an adult woman is hanging off the back of her man, but nonetheless, the looks are odd. I disengage and slide down Roman's back and reach for his hand.

"I feel like I missed something by keeping my eyes closed."

"You didn't," Lydia says. "It takes awhile for you to adjust to their speed, at least it did for me. The first time I kept my eyes open, I was sicker than a dog." She and Damen walk ahead.

Roman goes to follow, but I hold him back. "What is it?" he asks.

"Nothing. I just wanted a moment with you." He pulls me to him and kisses me lightly, and just like that, all seems right in my world.

Like a typical outing, I make Roman take picture after picture with me. Every time we stop to read a placard, I use the opportunity to capture the moment. And every time I start to get too hot, I pull my boyfriend close and use his cool temperature to cool down.

Boyfriend? Did I really call him my boyfriend? Yes, I did, and I really like the sound of it.

"Are you having fun?"

"I am, are you?" I ask him.

He nods and leans over the wall, spreading his arms wide.

"Please don't do that," I beg.

Roman stops and pulls me into his arms. "You do know, if I fell, I'd live."

I shrug. "I'm still learning."

"I'm invincible."

"Mhm..." I rest my head on his shoulder and let him hold me. Between the wind at my back and him, I shiver.

"I think you're the only one in Boulder City who is cold right now."

"You're my personal air conditioner."

Roman laughs. "I can be a lot more if you'd like." He tugs at the bottom of my earlobe. The simple act increases my body temperature, making me hot... for him.

After the dam, we drive to the lake where the vampire men have packed a lunch and plenty of water for Lydia and me. The men have decided to show off their strength by climbing up a deadly rock formation and diving into the lake. Admittedly, this act would kill a human, but not Roman and Damen. Nope, these two resurface without a single scratch on them.

Once we get back to the hotel, Roman hands his keys over to Damen and tells him he'll pick up the Jeep later. Roman and I walk, hand in hand, through the lobby and inside the elevator; I let him know with my mouth that I want him to stay. His hands are all over me, and mine is in his hair, tugging at the ends of his perfectly coifed strands.

Thank heavens Roman's senses are extraordinary because he moves me from the elevator to my door without missing a step. Somehow, I get my front door open, and we're inside without much effort.

"Roman..."

"Yes, Fiona," he whispers against my skin as his mouth abates my warm flesh. "I can smell your need for me."

"I'm sorry, what the fuck did you say?"

I push Roman away at the sound of my father's voice. He's standing in my foyer, his face red and his fist clenched. "Daddy," I say, scrambling to fix myself and pull away from Roman, but he doesn't budge. He lets out a low growl as he turns and looks over his shoulder. From this angle, I can see one of his fangs. "Roman?" my voice quivers.

"Get the hell away from my daughter." In my father's hand is a stake. Roman turns, shielding me. "Did you hear me, monster? You're not welcome here."

The grip Roman has on my hip tightens. "Roman, please."

"I will end you!" my dad yells. He rushes toward us with his arm raised and the stake heading toward Roman. In a flash, there's a deafening crash and a loud roar, followed by screaming. Roman's arms are around me, telling me everything's okay. I realize, I'm the one screaming and I don't know why.

I look at Roman, who seems pensive. Beyond me, there's a moan, and I turn to find my dad lying on the floor with blood coming from a cut on his forehead. "Daddy," I say, pushing away from Roman. "Dad, can you hear me?"

He moans. I glance over my shoulder at Roman. "What did you do?"

"He interrupted us," he says as if this is no big deal.

"So you try to kill him," I state, standing up. "That's my father, Roman. The man you so desperately want to do business with." Roman's eyes go from mine to my dad's and back to mine. I shake my head. "Roman, you have to leave."

"No, I should stay."

"You can't." I point to the door and look at the floor, unable to look Roman in the eyes. Once he leaves, I rush to the bathroom for my first aid kit. When I get back to my dad, he's standing and holding the back of his head.

"Sit down, let me take a look at your head."

"What the hell are you doing with a vampire, Fiona? You let that monster touch you."

I ignore him.

"Fiona!" He grabs my hand, stopping me from putting a piece of gauze on his forehead. "He's going to kill you, Fiona. He's a monster. They can't be trained to act like humans."

"I don't want to talk about this."

"Look at your wall and tell me that is normal." He jabs his finger toward my now shattered mirror and broken side table. "He tried to kill me because I walked in before he bit you. He was treating you like prey, not a human. I won't stand for this, Fiona. You know this."

My dad stands and abruptly walks by me, muttering something unintelligible. I jump when my door slams, leaving me with a heart that's about to beat out of my chest. I look over my shoulder at the mess where my dad landed against the wall, and let my tears fall. I knew Roman was too good to be true.

*W*ho the fuck just carries around a goddamn stake for killing vampires? It's not the fucking dark ages anymore. All I can think is that he's so crazy and misguided that he has never even met an actual vampire. What the fuck? When she insisted I leave, she wouldn't even make eye contact with me. I simply don't understand. Her father tries to kill me, completely unprovoked, but I have to leave? It's fucking ridiculous, and I'm seeing red.

I bolt in an instant, blowing down the stairwell and out the door without being seen. Utilizing the supernatural ability to leave quickly is the only thing that I knew to do. I haven't wanted to rip a human being to shreds in a hundred years. The way he attacked me filled me with such rage that my body temperature felt as though it had risen, which is completely impossible.

Practically flying, I get myself to Clutch and look for Selene. I don't say hello to anyone I recognize; I'm in no mood. When I find her, she is talking to some vampires I know, and I walk over and grab her arm, dragging her away.

"What the fuck, Roman?" She growls at me before hissing and showing her fangs.

"I need to talk to you."

"I can see that, but you don't get to manhandle me like that," she says, yanking her arm back. I'm beside myself with frustration and begin running my hands through my hair, pacing back and forth. "What the fuck is going on, Roman?"

"I had a situation tonight."

"That's obvious." She rolls her eyes and waves her hand, encouraging me to continue.

"Fiona's father tried to kill me," I blurt out.

"What? How the hell did this happen?" She looks around the room to see if anyone has heard us. She nods for me to follow her as she walks toward her office.

I sit in the chair across from her desk, exasperated. "Things were fine, or so I thought. Fiona and I went to Hoover Dam with Damen and Lydia. After, we went back to her apartment. I actually think that tonight was going to be the night she let me stay."

"Obviously that wasn't the case. Where does her father come in?" Selene leans back in her chair, arms crossed, looking at me intently. Run-ins with humans who want to kill you, is never good, and I know this.

"We were... kissing. And when we entered her house, her father was standing there and saw us. He flipped out, and came after me with a fucking stake."

Groaning, Selene buried her face in her hands. "Are you fucking kidding me?"

"Uh, no. No, I'm not."

"For fuck's sake. Then what? You didn't kill him, did you?" She leans over her desk, raising a perfectly manicured eyebrow at me condemningly.

"No, I didn't fucking kill him! It's not the 17th century for Christ's sake. I threw him into the wall, which of course ended up being far more dramatic than it probably needed to be. There was a large mirror and a table there which all smashed, and he fell to the ground." I am experiencing a range of emotions from rage, to frustration, to concern over Fiona's well being. Letting out a sigh, I hang my head and lean forward, resting my elbows on my lap.

"How did Fiona respond?" she asks calmly.

"She told me to leave."

"I see. And this clearly upsets you. So, what do you want from me, Roman? She's your consort; your problem. You can't throw humans into fucking walls though, or you're going to create attention where it's not needed, and certainly not wanted. I don't want a visit from the Sisters, do you? I'm not about our creators coming to town to rain down their punishment for this." She was stern and narrowed her green eyes at me.

"Of course I don't. I get it, Selene. It was an accident. I knew her dad hated vampires, we've been down that road. But I didn't know he'd be carrying a fucking wooden stake with him to just stab a vampire any old fucking time. I was caught off guard. I haven't been attacked by a human in a hundred and fifty years."

She relaxes again and leans back in her chair with a thoughtful expression. "Okay, okay. You're right. Nobody expects to get staked on a date these days. He sounds like a real piece of work." She rolls her eyes as she says it. "So, I presume you're here because you're upset over Fiona, and you want my advice?"

"Yes, Sherlock, how astute of you." I roll my eyes right back at her. "That's exactly what I want. You've been my friend for centuries. How do I fix this?"

"Stop fucking pursuing humans who don't come along willingly would be my best advice."

"That's not an option here. I need her." I catch myself before saying that I love her. I know it seems like a crazy thing to say or to feel. I've never tasted her. She doesn't take that fucking cross off. But she lets me in emotionally. Her heart is kind. Her innocence and her desire to understand me draws me in.

"Ugh." She groans at me. "Look, I think you should stay the fuck away from her. But I can see that's not going to happen, so the only solution I can think of is that you need to bring her here. She needs to see what our life is really like. Right now, all she sees is the work you've done to seem human. But you're not fucking human. I don't think she fully understands what she's dealing with."

"She knows I'm a vampire, Selene."

"Uh huh. But does she even know what that means? She knows you're a man, who has fangs. Those are just fucking teeth. Not being able to hear your heartbeat is just the tip of the iceberg. Has she seen you feed? Have you bitten her? Has she experienced the vampire life? Or did she get the vampire who acts like a human to fit in?" she asks before pressing her lips together and glaring at me.

Fuck. Selene is totally right. I've spent all of my time trying to show Fiona how human I am. I'm not human. I'm not the monster her father says that I am, but I'm never going to be something I'm not, mortal. I realize that my strategy of covering up what I am to show her my humanity has perhaps backfired.

"So you think she needs to come here?" I furrow my brows. I'm skeptical that a feeding bar and lounge is the absolute best idea under the circumstances.

"It doesn't sound like the greatest day of my life, but for

you, it's the only way to see if she can handle the truth. I don't enjoy entertaining humans who are leery of our kind or of our ways, or that come here begrudgingly like we're some kind of a sideshow. We've been through that era, and I'd just as soon forget that we were almost all staked to death over what we are." She pauses and takes a deep sigh before continuing. "However, for you, for my partner in this immortal life, I suggest that you bring her here. If she can handle what she sees and experiences, then maybe you can salvage something from this relationship if you want to call it that. But let me ask you something, Roman."

"What's that?"

"Why her? You could have practically any woman on this earth. What makes her so special that you're willing to stick your neck out for her? You'll outlive her a thousand times over. What's the point?" I knew this line of questioning would come eventually. Selene never believed in settling down with humans or settling down at all really. We'd talked about it before over the years when we'd seen vampires marry humans, and live with them until they died. She'd made it very clear that for her there was no point in getting attached to a creature who would age and die. I had agreed with her for many years, that is until I met Fiona.

"I can't describe it. It is a gut feeling, and instinct. I'm drawn to her in a way that is almost primal; I couldn't stop it even if I wanted to."

"So, she's your prey?" Selene suggested with a smirk.

"No! It's not like that at all. Do you even listen to me? I want to protect her. Take care of her." My thoughts retreated to the expression on her face when she looked at me in her house. She had disgust, and fear in her eyes. I had to fix this.

Again, Selene rolls her eyes. "Whatever you say,

Roman. I don't get it, but I'll help you. However, I can. Bring her here so she can see how the other half lives. If she's got the stomach for it, you'll know in an instant whether or not this can work. That's the only way you'll know."

"Thank you, Selene."

"You're welcome. And while we're at it – keep your fucking nose clean moving forward. Don't be throwing any more humans around. I'm serious!" She points her long pale finger at me aggressively as I get up to walk out. I nod my head in agreement and head back out the bar.

Deciding to try and talk to Fiona, I pull out my phone, dialing her number. I'm not surprised when my call goes to voicemail; I'm assuming she's just not taking my calls. I decide to hang around Clutch for awhile; I'm not ready to go home and sulk. Going back to her place seems like a bad idea, so I lament in public alone at the bar until the vampire sitting next to me with his consort, a lovely, young, brunette human who I've seen here before, addresses me.

"Hey, are you Roman?" he asks me with hesitation in his voice.

"Yea, why?"

He turns on his stool to face me, then glances around the room to see if anyone is listening. We're vampires, anyone could be listening, and they don't have to be sitting anywhere near us to hear, so I impatiently wait to find out what he wants.

"We were just walking through the Glacier Palace Casino on Broad Street before coming here, and uh... I think your consort is there."

Now he's garnered my full attention. "What was she doing there?" I ask brusquely. I'm annoyed.

"Well, she was drinking; a lot. And we could, well I

could, hear her talking about you to a bartender there. I wasn't really eavesdropping so much as she was pretty upset about a vampire, and then she said your name. She seems pretty mad about whatever happened."

Not knowing this vamp, I had no intention of getting into my business with him, but I was grateful to know where I could find her and to hear that she wasn't with her father. I decide to go to her immediately.

"Thank you..." I trail off, not knowing his name.

"Boris." He sticks his hand out to shake mine.

"Boris. Thank you." I get up and walk out abruptly, headed straight for Glacier. It's close to Clutch, in the more vampire friendly section of town, so I walk quickly, listening intently, trying to get a read on her voice. It can be difficult at times to pick up the voices that you're trying to hear, particularly when your own mind is racing, but within a few moments, I can hear her.

"I thought he was different. I guess my daddy was right. Humans and vamps just don't mix," I hear her say as I near the entrance. I know she doesn't believe this, she can't.

Before I advance, I watch her for a moment. She's talking to a female bartender, who happens to be a vampire. You can't see her mark, it's covered up with a leather cuff, and I wonder if Fiona has any idea that she's talking about her problems with her vampire boyfriend to another vampire. Yes, boyfriend. That's what I am in human speak. She's mine, and I am hers. While I may use different terminology in my culture, it's the same thing, and it's time to go reclaim her.

The vampire at the bar is bleached blonde, with a provocatively low cut tank top, and senses me coming before I arrive. As she makes eyes at me, I shift my glance and nod my head away from Fiona, indicating that she is mine and that my Fiona is no human conquest for her tonight. Vampires are territorial and do not go after each other's consorts, once a relationship has been established. There are plenty of willing humans to choose from, but should we choose just one to be ours, respect for that is expected among our kind. Understanding, she smiles at Fiona and walks to help other patrons at the bar, leaving Fiona alone with her drink.

I know I need to talk to her now. I'm nervous, and quite certain that if I were human, my palms would be sweating. Thank the fates that I don't sweat or have a heartbeat because it would be thumping right out of my chest. As I approach her, I can smell her perfume, her perfect Fiona scent and it fills me with desire for her.

"Fiona?" I take the seat next to her.

"How did you find me, Roman?" She refuses to make eye contact with me. Before I have a chance to answer, she continues. "Oh, that's right, with your superhuman senses. Well, what do you want?" She takes a sip of her drink and licks her bottom lip, where a small drop of liquid has remained.

I swallow hard, watching her before I reply. "I want to talk to you. I need to talk to you."

She turns to face me, and I see immediately that her eyes are red, likely from crying. "I don't think there's anything left to talk about, Roman. You threw my dad against a wall. Not only that but with superhuman strength, leaving a humanly sized indent on my wall. You could have killed him!"

It's impossible to defend my actions, but I try. "Fiona, your father could have killed me with that stake. I was defending myself. If I wanted him dead, he'd be dead."

Her mouth drops open in shock at my blunt statement.

This is what Selene was talking about. Fiona needs to be reminded that I'm a fucking vampire. Yes, I have super strength; I have predatory tendencies, and that won't change. It's what I am, and it's time to stop hiding it.

"Wow Roman, really?" She shakes her head at me.

"Fiona, listen to me." I wait for her to look back at me with her full attention. "I am not a human."

"I know that, Roman." She looks at me, confused and annoyed.

"Do you? Because I think that you need to understand that I will give you the world, but I am not a regular mortal man. There is a part of my life you need to see for yourself. You need to understand what being a vampire really means."

"You answer my questions all the time. I know what being a vampire is about. I get it. You didn't have to handle things that way today. I cared about you," she says, blowing me off.

Her use of the past tense cared, stings. Taking a chance, I rest my hand on her thigh gently. "Fiona, I don't think you do. You've just barely scratched the surface. Will you come with me?"

"Come with you where?" she asks hesitantly.

"I want you to come to Clutch. I've told you about it. I want you to see what my life is about, and what being a part of my life means. Please?" I can see the hesitation on her face. She's trying to read my expression before she makes a decision, but I can sense her want for me. "Fiona, I care about you. I will fix things with your father. But I need for you to understand what I truly am."

"You won't let anything happen to me? Like nobody gets to bite me, right?" Her hand draws up to the cross she's still wearing.

It's against the rules to enter the club if you're not willing to get bitten, although it's not really enforced. I've never seen anyone turned away over it since that's what most humans go there for anyway. "You are mine, Fiona. No one gets to touch you except me." My hand slides up her thigh a bit, and I can feel her heart rate increase.

"I want to understand, Roman." She rests her hand on mine and meets my gaze. "I'll go, but I'm still upset over today. I'm mad at both you and my father."

Relief washes over me, and I throw some cash on the bar for her tab and pull her with me as I stand up. She immediately softens into me for a hug, and as I hold her tightly, I realize that I am in love with her. Whatever it takes, I'm going to make this work.

We make our way back to Clutch, and at the door, we're greeted by Corban, who immediately notices Fiona's cross around her neck.

"She can't wear that in here," he addresses me, and points to her neck.

"She's with me," I reply.

"That may be the case, but she can't wear that."

I turn to Fiona and hope for the best. "Fiona? I need you to take the cross off."

"What? No."

"Listen to me. No one is going to touch you except me."

"But they could compel me. And I don't want that. I want to know everything I'm doing. I don't want to be controlled." She seems scared, like she's going to run.

I take her face in my hands and look deeply into her eyes. "Fiona, listen to me. You're mine. I wouldn't compel you with or without the cross, and I won't let anyone else. This is important if you want to understand my culture. I need you to comply. Willingly." I take a step back, hoping she makes the right decision and to my surprise, she does.

Slowly, she reaches around the back of her neck and unhooks the chain reluctantly. She drops the cross in her small purse, then looks back up at me with a smile. I can see her resolve now, and it fills me with pleasure. I lean in to kiss her softly, her lips tasting sweeter than ever, then I take her hand and smirk at Corban, who's now opened the door for us to enter Clutch.

16

FIONA

*U*nlike at Hoover Dam, Roman doesn't tell me to close my eyes when we step into his hangout, his lair full of blood sucking, human killing friends who are passing by us in a blur. My grip on Roman's hand tightens, but I don't feel secure. It's not enough. I need him to shield me from his brotherhood.

We're not three or four steps in when Roman pauses. I don't know if this is for dramatic effect or what, but color me underwhelmed. I've seen enough. I don't belong here, especially without my cross. My hand reaches for my neck, and I close my eyes, wishing I hadn't agreed to this.

Nevertheless, I'm here, as promised so I can try to understand who Roman is when we're not together. I need to keep an open mind because I truly like Roman, although, after his mishap with my father, I don't know if we'll be able to be together. I know my father well enough to know he's going to make me choose, Roman or him, and by him, my father means my trust fund.

The club is dark with red and black accents every-where. It's exactly what I would expect a vampire den to look like. Clearly, whoever owns this place didn't branch out from their known color palette. It wouldn't hurt the vampire community to add a little cream or yellow to their lives. Although, I supposed red and black mean you don't see any blood stains.

Roman takes my hand and leads us to the bar. It seems like it's a mile long and completely out of place.

"I thought you don't drink."

"I don't... we don't."

"Yet, you have a fully stocked bar, and people have drinks in their hands."

"Those are humans."

I look down the bar at the men and women saddled up to it. Each person has a different expression on his or her face. The man next to us looks sad, almost as if he's lost his job, and the woman three seats down is surveying the room, possibly looking for a man? It's hard to tell. "Why are they here?"

"Mostly, because they prefer this lifestyle."

"You mean being bitten?"

"It's not always about biting, Fiona."

"Then what's it about, Roman?"

"It's about having a deeper connection with another being. It's about helping someone survive. It's about finding your place in the world."

I take his words to heart; especially what he said first, the deeper connection. I know I feel something for Roman that isn't forced or a result of him biting me. I genuinely like being with him.

"What would the human like to drink?" I suck in a breath at the sight of the woman in front of me. Everything about her is flawless from her long dark hair, perfectly curved figure, sharp green eyes and her boobs... yes, I'm marveling at her chest and the way her breasts are cupped flawlessly in her red (no less) corset. And her fangs. Her tongue runs over them as she looks at me. I swallow hard, and my body goes on high alert.

"Selene, this is my Fiona. Fiona, this is Selene, she owns the Las Vegas Clutch."

I extend my hand, but she doesn't shake it. Instead, she's throwing the proverbial dagger at Roman, which is something I'll have to ask him about later.

"May I have water, please?" My throat's dry and I've had enough liquor for the evening. I need to keep my wits about myself, especially in here.

"Water?' Selene nods and places a glass in front of me so fast I don't even see her move to fill it up. Tentatively, I take a sip, not sure what to expect.

"Thank you." I'm still alive, at least for the moment. For all I know, this is a trap, and I'm here to be turned... wait, can vampires do that, turn humans into vampires without their permission? I don't remember in any of my readings, and the thought literally has me shaking in my seat.

"Hey, are you okay?" Roman's hand is on my back. I nod, but I can see he doesn't believe me. "What's going on?"

"Did you bring me here so you can turn me into a vampire?" I whisper. Suddenly the room goes eerily quiet, and the only thing I can hear is my own heartbeat. I'm afraid to look anywhere except at Roman, out of fear there's an entire coven of undead beings approaching me. Do they all take turns? Will they strap me down and drain my blood? God, I should've read more before I ever agreed to go on a date with Roman.

"Fiona, it's against the law for us to turn anyone."

I glance over my shoulder to find about eight or so vampires looking rather hungry. "What're they doing?"

"Kiss me, Fiona. They think you're here on your own and are willing to be with them."

Roman doesn't give me a chance to understand what he's said before his lips are on mine. Without hesitation, my hand goes to his hair, and I pull him closer, needing to not only taste him but also feel him pressed against me. There are a few mumbles behind us, and the music has started back up. When Roman pulls away from me, I feel the loss of him instantly. "Can I show you around?"

I nod and take his hand as I slide down from the barstool. The deeper we walk into the recess of the club, the tighter my grip is on his hand. Not because of what I see, it's because of who's looking at me, eyes everywhere with intense stares that cause the fine hairs on my arms to rise.

In the back of the club is a dance floor. Half clothed bodies gyrate, people make-out and I swear I see a couple having sex. The vampire male looks up from his consort and winks before disappearing. I strain my head to try and see where they went, but to no avail.

Roman pulls back a black curtain and motions for me to step through. "Back here is where you can go for some privacy."

"Like sex?"

He shrugs. "Yes, but also for feedings. Some humans don't want others to watch. Plus, this is where the um..."

"Juice hustlers?"

"No, we call them prostitutes just like you, and contrary to popular belief, we don't need to bite our partner to achieve an orgasm. The act only heightens the experience for everyone involved. Anyway, this is where they work."

"Do you want to watch a feeding?"

I shake my head but stop quickly. "I don't know, do I?"

"It's only something you can answer, Fiona. I won't make you do anything you don't want to do."

"What if someone wants to feed off me?"

"Absolutely not," Roman says. "I won't allow it."

"What if I want it?"

"Then you don't want me. I don't share, Fiona. You're not some shiny toy I want to pass around."

"But you share these women," I point out.

"That's different. The mindset is different."

"I see." Except, I don't. "Do you sleep with the women here?"

I think if Roman could breathe, he'd let out an exasperated sigh right about now. "In the past, yes, but not since I've met you."

A vampire and an overly giggly woman brush past, taking the room right behind us. They don't bother to shut the curtain, letting anyone passing by watch what they're about to do. He kisses her, groping her breast and grinding against her. His mouth leaves her and trails toward her neck.

Her eyes flash open, and then a soft, satisfying smile appears. She looks elated that he's sucking the life right out of her. Completely content with what's going on. I look away and place my hand on my stomach, waiting for dinner to work its way back up.

"They're together," Roman says.

"How can you tell?

"Vampires see bonds between a vampire and a human consort. If another vampire were to bite her, her mate has every right to kill the other. He'd likely kill his mate too for betraying him."

"So what you're telling me is, if you bite me, I can only be with you."

"No, bonds can be broken. They just don't happen often."

"I feel like there are so many rules, and yet I know none of them." I turn and leave Roman in the hallway, I make it about three feet before Roman's chest is pressed against my back and his arm is around my waist. His lips trail from my collarbone to my ear, in a languid motion. Each kiss meant to turn me on.

"Dance with me, Fiona."

It's not a request, but a demand. A damn sexy one at that. Roman leads us to the dance floor and starts moving our bodies to the beat. I can feel his need for me growing, and I find myself pushing into him. His mouth is everywhere along the back of my neck, and his hands move freely along my body, massaging my breasts. As I look around, I expect people to stare, to gawk, but they're all focused on whoever they're with. No one here gives a shit what the other person is doing, and I find myself not caring that Roman is dry humping me in the middle of a crowded bar. There's something seriously wrong with me right now.

Roman's hand snakes under my blouse, and his ice-cold hand gropes my breast. I lean into him, turning my head. "Not here, Roman. Not like this in front of everyone."

"Your home is not safe for me. Can I take you to mine?"

"Are there coffins?"

His laughter vibrates against me. "No, darling. There are no coffins, bats or any of the other folklore you may have read."

"What about faeries and werewolves?"

Roman stops moving. I turn in his arms and place my hands on his cheeks. "Roman?"

After a long minute, he winks. "You read too many books."

17

ROMAN

*S*wiftly, I take us to my home, which isn't far from hers. In front of my door, she leans into my back as I insert the key into the lock. I can sense her anticipation as well as her reservation; she knows why we're here. She knows what we're about to do. Her hands are running along my sides, teasing me. In one smooth motion, I pull her into my arms, cross over the threshold and slam the door, pressing her against it.

"Roman," she breathes out as I press my body against hers, my hands roaming, touching everywhere they can before she tells me to stop.

"Fiona, do you want this?" I ask again, needing her assurance. I won't make her do anything she doesn't want, and I need her to tell me what she wants, what her desires are.

As I snake my tongue along her jaw, inhaling her scent, she lets out a slight gasp. Her body is warm and soft; she melts into me. "I want you, Roman," she whispers.

I step away, grabbing her hand, pulling her across the open layout of my home toward the bedroom. She glances around the room, probably looking for something that screams vampire, which I find mildly amusing. She's been fed a lot of garbage propaganda about vampires, which is clear.

"Do you need anything?" I ask her before we reach my master suite.

Without a word, she shakes her head. I pause for a moment, just taking her in. She's beautiful, and even though I'm not her first, there's an innocence behind her eyes I can't get enough of. I pull her to me for a kiss. It's slow and soft at first but escalates quickly as she slides her tongue along my teeth, gently biting my lower lip. I can't resist any longer and use my abilities, I launch us to the bed. We lay side by side, and while she looks startled at first for a moment, she quickly smiles and begins to plant kisses on my neck. Her movements are fluid and sensual. With nimble fingers, Fiona begins to unbutton my shirt with one hand.

I roll over, caging her beneath me, propped on my arms and take her in again. I need to make sure there's no apprehension before this happens. Once I bite her, we'll be bonded for the rest of her life or until either of us sever the bond. As if she's reading my mind, she says, "I want you to bite me tonight, Roman."

A grin spreads across my face knowing she can see my fangs now. The anticipation of biting her, of tasting her blood for the first time is almost too much to bear. My cock becomes harder and presses against my jeans almost painfully. "I won't hurt you, Fiona," I promise.

"I know you won't." She pulls me toward her for a kiss.

I do plan to bite her tonight, drinking her in. I fully intend to finally satiate my thirst for her. But first, I need her to let go. I want to pleasure her, I need her to come undone for me. Our kiss becomes more passionate, and I can feel she's ready for me to lead this moment. Without wasting any more time, I gently pull her up to her knees with me on the bed, staring into her eyes. She waits for me to undress her with expectancy. A slight coy smile forms across her lips as she watches me take the hem of her shirt and slide it up and over her head. It's times like these when I wish I were human so I could remember what it felt like to gasp at the woman in front of me with her beautiful breasts and soft curves.

Her heart is beating faster than normal, forcing the blood through her body like rapids, and I swallow hard at the thought of her blood trickling down my throat. She's wearing an insanely sexy black bra with lace that barely covers her tight nipples, which I have no doubt desire my attention. Fiona runs her hands along my chest, kissing and nipping at me, leaving me no choice but to finish what she started. Instead of working the buttons of my shirt, I rip it from my body and throw the remnants onto my bedroom floor.

My need for her grows. I need her beneath me, on top of me, anywhere gravity allows. I scoop her into my arms, laying her down, and practically rip her pants off. This lead up is making me insane, and when I see her lying on my bed in nothing but her sexy lingerie, I'm done moving slow. I'd done being patient. Moving on top of her, I slide the strap of her bra down, revealing the pale pink nipple of her breast and run the pad of my thumb over it, causing her breath to hitch. I do the same to the other before taking one into my mouth, rolling my tongue around it. She moans in pleasure, grabbing my hair and bucks her hips slightly. Her hands are frenzied, trying to get my pants undone. I do my best to help her, but honestly, I'm too focused on getting her remaining garment off. I want her naked and spread out on my bed, ready for the feast. Fiona manages to get my pants pushed over my hips, and my cock free.

If Fiona has any qualms about what's about to happen, she doesn't say a word. Instead, she wraps her legs around me, looking up at me through her lashes. "You're beautiful, Fiona; I want you so badly."

"Take me, Roman; I'm yours," she whispers through heavy breaths. So I do. I make her mine.

For a man who never has to blink and who has to force himself to have human habits, there's nothing making my eyes roll back into my head except for the pure unadulterated pleasure I feel having Fiona wrapped around me. She rocks against me, urging me to make love to her. Who the hell am I to deny this woman? I've wanted her, courted her and finally have her in my bed, and yet I'm frozen, unable to move. Her feather light kisses bring me to my senses, and my hips start thrusting forward, pushing deeply into her core. We make love, exploring each other, being one with each other.

"I want to feed you, Roman."

I'm so lost in her, I don't ask for confirmation but pull back to look in her eyes. She nods at me with no apprehension, and I bare my fangs to her. Her eyes light up, and her legs tighten around me as I move in on her neck. Before I allow my animal instinct to kick in, I drag my tongue along the spot I intend to leave my mark upon her pristine flesh. Still making love, her nails dig into my sides as I sink my teeth in and she cries out, freezing up as I start to drink her in.

Her pain lasts only a moment, and as her body softens, I pull her tight to me. I failed to mention to her that the initial pain would subside quickly, as the saliva from a vampire paralyzes the nerve endings around a bite. She begins to moan loudly, rocking into me, as I'm latched onto her, the warm blood coating my throat as I drink. Her nails dig deeper, and she begins to climax under me. Her sounds become louder, and when she screams my name out, I let go as well, finishing with her and watching a small drop of blood stream down her neck from each of the holes I've caused.

Still panting, she comes down from the high and meets my gaze. "That only hurt for a second," she says, sounding surprised.

"I know, baby," I reply, smiling. I lean down to lick up the blood that's escaped my bite mark and savor the sweetness. I've said to her several times that feeding isn't erotic, but that's not entirely true. With someone you have an emotional attachment, it's the most sensual and intense connection possible.

I roll to the side and inspect where I bit her closely, before taking her hand in mine and bringing it to my lips. With her other hand, she touches the bite and inspects her fingertips. "I'm not bleeding?" she asks.

"No, sweetheart. You won't bleed afterward." I wait for more questions, but she remains silent. "Are you all right?" I ask.

Letting out a slight laugh, she turns on her side to face me. "I'm fucking great. How about you?"

I can't help but to laugh; that isn't the response I was expecting. Somehow I thought she'd have more questions, or would want to talk about mechanics of the moment or something. She continues to be full of surprises.

"I'm good, Fiona. That was amazing." Not only was the sex incredible, we fit together so incredibly well, in sync with each other's needs, but her blood is magnificent. I could taste the slightest bit of the alcohol she'd had tonight, but it was all I had hoped it would be. I wasn't quite ready for a feeding. I typically wait until I have to feed, but drinking from her was like having an extravagant dessert.

"Was it? Am I delicious?" she asks, completely serious.

I want to laugh. I've never been asked a more hilarious question in all my life, but she means it with such innocence, I don't dare mock it. Instead, I bring her face to mine and plant a small kiss on her lips. "I could never get enough of you, Fiona. You're the most exquisite thing I have ever tasted in my life."

Seemingly pleased with my answer, she smiles and rests her head on my chest. While I stroke her hair, I think about what's next. I want to enjoy the moment, relish in it. But I know we've got many hurdles to overcome, and the sooner we handle them, the better. I know it's not the time to discuss it, so I lie there, holding the woman I'm definitely in love with, listening to her breathe.

"Roman, how often can we do that?" she asks, still resting on me.

"Do what, sweetheart?"

"How often can you bite me without killing me?"

I don't want her to think I could ever kill her, but it's actually a good question. There have been accidents in the past, where a vampire and his or her consort didn't manage the vampire's thirst properly, and things got out of hand. "We wouldn't want to do it every day. It would make you too weak. I don't need to feed every day anyway," I explain.

"I don't want you to feed on anyone else anymore," she says quietly.

"I wouldn't dream of it," I squeeze her, brimming with satisfaction. She's mine now. She wants to be mine.

"I don't think this is going to be easy for us, Roman."

"No, I don't suppose that it is," I reply with as little

emotion as possible. I know she's referring to her father, who I'd just as soon kill after our initial introduction than work with at this point, but I'm aware of human relationships and their importance.

Silence falls between us, and as I wait for her to fall asleep, she squeezes me. "That was really fucking good." She chuckles.

Unable to help myself, and happy that our conversation had lightened up a bit, for now, I reply. "There's a lot more where that came from, babe. You're mine now, and I'm going to worship you."

She lets out a sigh, and I can feel that sleep is taking over her body. I wait patiently, enjoying the moment, satisfied with the end of an incredibly rocky day.

18

FIONA

*G*rowing up, I spent my summers with my grandparents, working at their campground. My job was to run the general store under the watchful eye of my grandma. I used to love checking the campers in and helping them with their inner tubes and kayak rentals. There was one family in particular who I waited for every year. They had a son two years older than me, but sometimes we'd hang out on the swing set together or get some ice cream when the ding dong cart would drive by.

The year I turned thirteen, I swore I was going to kiss him. I was determined to be carefree and enjoy my first summer as a teenager. His name was Charlie, he was so cute, and by the end of the summer, he had this fantastic tan. I remember waiting for his family to show up, and when they didn't, I checked the books to see if they had a reservation and nothing. My grandma didn't know why they chose not to come back. It indeed wasn't the first time this had happened.

Still, the next year I waited and the year after that. It

wasn't until I was eighteen and spending my last summer working at the camp that Charlie showed up, this time with a wife and a baby. I feigned recognition of him, even though I knew who he was as soon as he stepped out of his car. I wanted to ask him what happened, find out why they stopped coming, but it wasn't my place. Any feelings I had for him were long gone, plus he had a wife.

It was as if things hadn't changed. At night, Charlie was on the swing set all by himself, and when I sat down, he started telling me what had happened. A vampire had killed his mother, and his father was jailed for crimes against inhumanity. He had to go live with his aunt, which meant the end of his trips here. I couldn't believe what I was hearing because surely the laws were in place to protect humans. We had vampires staying at the campground and never had any issues. None of this made sense to me.

When I went back home at the end of summer, I told my father, who detailed horror stories of vampires and how they kill humans for fun. Little did I know, Charlie's parents were friends of my dad's, and my father took the death and subsequent imprisonment of his friend rather hard. He told me I was never ever to associate with the undead, under any circumstances.

My circumstances have changed. Sure, I could've told Roman to leave me alone, to stay away or find some voodoo bullshit to banish him from my life, but I didn't. Not because I'm in the business of pissing off my father, but because I like Roman. I like him a lot. The only downfall is he's a vampire, and while I don't mind it, others in my circle do and will. Being with him is going to cost me.

How much, I'm not sure, but I'm willing to take the gamble so to speak. I don't think my father will disown me as he says because I have too much dirt on him. I could destroy his empire with one phone call. He may think of me as a tart, an airhead he employs to bring in business, but my notes are meticulous and damaging.

Then there's Leslie. Once she finds out I've slept with Roman, our friendship is over for sure. Thing is, I can't let her find out, not just yet, and I also can't keep ignoring her because she's liable to show up at my apartment, and when I don't answer the door, there will be a barrage of questions, like where have you been.

At Roman's, being thoroughly fucked. I can easily say I'm a proud member of the once you go vamp, you never go back club, and will be leading the charge as president. Lana did not go into detail about what sex is like with a vampire. Although come to think of it, I doubt I would either. There's no way I'm sharing details of what Roman and I do in his bedroom.

The black scarf I tied around my neck hides the leftover bruising. It's faint but still visible, and today I'd rather not comment on my sex life. Over the silk material, my fingers rub where the marks have healed, closing my eyes as I recall the moment Roman's fangs sunk into my skin.

The instant rush of adrenaline was something I've never felt before. My fight or flight kicked in, and I chose to stay, and let him feed on my vein. Of course, the fact that he was deeply embedded inside of me, making me feel like nothing I've ever felt before did help the situation. Having him fill me, stretch me to encase his girth has left me yearning for more. It's all we've done for the past few days, in every room of his house, on every surface. I've let him command me, control me, and in return, he's given me the most delicious orgasms of my life. The biting put me over the edge; giving me this endorphin I didn't know existed. I'm addicted, and I want more.

Thankfully, I won't be the only person in hundred degree weather trying to cover up. It's a common thing these days, but still not favorable to a lot of humans. Without a doubt, I will get stares and snickers, and you know what sucks to be the person not on the receiving end. Giving myself to Roman has been the most glorious thing I have ever done. Lana's right; don't knock it until you try it.

Before leaving my bathroom, I make sure my cross is centered between my breasts. I still wear it and plan to continue doing so. It doesn't bother Roman, and it's not like it keeps my virtue intact, and he should never have any reason to compel me. The only place I can't wear it is at Clutch. Roman knows I'm still unsure of his hang out, but have promised him we'd go because it's really the only place we can be free without people commenting or staring at us in disgust.

Downstairs at the pool, my two best friends wait for me. Already, I can sense the tension between them. Since Lana's admission of sleeping with the vampire at her gym, she and Leslie have been at odds. Maybe having lunch with them today is a mistake, although I do look hot in the new outfit Roman bought for me. It's like he knew I needed the new Lanvin hat and matching scarf, which is perfect for today because there's no hiding the bruising or explaining it as anything other than what it is, a bite mark. Groaning internally, I take uneasy steps toward the table where they're sitting. I hate feeling like I have something to hide, even though I do.

"Good afternoon, ladies." I sit and purposely leave my ensemble intact. It's not exactly kosher, but I'm all about change these days.

"Is that the new Lanvin?" Leslie asks.

I nod. "It is. Did you know Olivier Lapidus took over?

His design eye is simply amazing." When Roman presented me with this wide-brimmed hat, I thought he was joking. The demand is incredible, and unless you go to France, getting one stateside is extremely hard. I asked Roman if he went to France while I slept, and he laughed, telling me that despite his ability to move lightning fast, he couldn't, much to his chagrin, walk on or through the water. He would have to fly or take a boat like an ordinary human.

"Your sunglasses are new too. Did your father give you a raise?" Leslie wants to know. She's right about the sunglasses, but they were a gift last week from Roman, not yesterday. He gave me the Dolce and Gabbana's the same day he tried to kill me with the flowers.

"Someone has a beau," Lana says, making me wish I had told her beforehand. Honestly, I don't know why I didn't. Maybe it's because I want to keep Roman to myself, enjoy him a little before we have to play the couples game. It's okay going out with Lydia and Damen because they're like us, but Lana isn't serious about her vamp, at least not that I know of.

"No, nothing like that," I say, feeling about three feet tall for lying. I'd love to stand on top of the table and shout that I'm falling in love with Roman, who oddly enough doesn't have a surname name. I asked Lydia how that works and she said she's known as Lydia, wife of Damen. Nothing more is needed when it comes to their laws. Also, there isn't a single vampire in the world with the same name. Color me shocked.

"Wait, you tried those on the other day when we went shopping," Lana says.

"You went shopping without me?" Leslie looks hurt, precisely what I wanted to avoid.

"We ran into each other," I lie, and hate myself for

doing so. I look at Lana and wish she could see my eyes as I plead with her to shut her mouth. I'm not in the business of hurting Leslie, at least not on purpose. "I went back and bought them."

"Daddy's black American Express getting a workout, huh?"

"Something like that," I smirk at Lana, thinking I should've sat closer to her so I could kick her for being a bitch right now.

The waitress appears, wearing a scarf. I want to laugh, but the realization on Leslie's face is anything but a joke. She looks from her to me, and it's like I can see the wheels spinning slowly in her head.

"Is this a new trend? I must've missed it." She picks up her phone and starts pressing the screen rapidly, undoubtedly surfing through one of her many fashion magazines, looking for this current fad.

"What can I get you, ladies?" the waitress asks, wholly disenchanted with Leslie's issue.

"I'll have the Cobb salad and iced tea, please," I tell her.

"Same," says Lana.

"I'll have..." Leslie flips through the menu, one she's seen well over twenty times in the past month, to decide. Leslie finally orders, but it isn't without some fanfare. She wants a cobb salad as well, but everything has to be on the side. It's only after the waitress has left, does she look at me. "I shouldn't have ordered."

"Um... why not? We're here to have lunch," I point out.

Leslie folds her hands on top of the table and looks in my direction, at least I think she is, but I can't tell for sure because of her sunglasses. "The trend says this is a new fashion for women to wear if they've been bitten by a... I can't even bring myself to say the word. Anyway, they're calling the new line of scarves, Once Bitten. I find it funny you have their number one seller."

I swallow hard at her statement and begin to laugh. I figure if I play it off as a coincidence, she'll be none the wiser.

"You got bit, didn't you? Did you sleep with that sexy vamp I met?" My mouth goes dry at Lana's outburst. Right now, I want to crawl under the table and hide, while simultaneously beating the crap out of Lana and her big mouth.

Leslie's eyes go wide and as much as I'd love to deny everything, I can't. I won't. I sit up in my chair a little straighter and look at Leslie, knowing either my friendship or my life is about to end because she'll inevitably tell my father.

"You can't even admit it, can you?" she asks.

"No, I can. I was choosing to keep my love life private. Unlike some of us." I glance quickly at Lana, who shrugs.

"I'm so disgusted by you, Fiona. I thought you were better than this, better than her." She points to Lana, who doesn't seem shocked by Leslie's outburst.

"I'm sorry you feel this way."

Leslie stands and moves rather quickly, gathering her stuff. She pauses when she steps by me, but eventually continues toward the exit. Breathing a sigh of relief would be nice right about now, but my heart is beating out of my chest at the unknown.

"How was it?"

"I'm sorry, what?"

Lana leans forward. "Tell me every dirty detail."

So I do, right there in the middle of the restaurant for everyone to hear.

19

ROMAN

*E*xquisite. Luscious. Delectable. Utterly tantalizing. All words I have used to describe Fiona in the last few days. Not only have I never tasted anything – anyone, as utterly delicious as her, but she has me hooked on her in every way. I'm an addict who spends most of my time thinking about her, waiting to get another fix.

After our first time together, the first time she let me bite her, I laid with her, watching her sleep. Thinking about how I'd come to be in this moment, feeling as I do, after all of these years. I don't remember any specifics about my life before turning, but I recall having human emotions. That's how I know it's love. It's a feeling, an inability to imagine life, or whatever it is I'm living, without her in it. I've roamed the earth, doing what and with whom I pleased, for as long as I can remember, and now I know why. It was to find Fiona.

While I have to feed on humans to survive, I've never felt a deep or spiritual connection to them on any level. I've always thought we were put on the earth together to each serve a purpose, with their use being to nourish our bodies. Defining my own path never even occurred to me until the last fifty years or so, when Selene and I were traveling through London, and discussing where to go next. We've lived much like tourists through our existence. Visiting the great cathedrals in Italy, including the Vatican when no one was looking, touring the Caribbean and lounging on the beach, spending our time looking for somewhere to build what could be considered the semblance of normalcy. I don't think we knew that's what we were doing. We were just enjoying our freedom, searching for the next part-time venue.

But what I didn't realize until now, was a normal life was fundamentally a mortal life. As vampires, we don't have to rest. We have places to feed around the world. At the heart of it all, we want for nothing. We are creatures of pleasure if we so choose. But the life of luxury, the reward of immortality, becomes empty once you've tasted the freedoms of travel, money and gratuitous sex around the globe. Before the laws were enacted, we didn't need to ask to feed, and we could take the blood of whom we chose, perhaps even their life when we saw fit. Certainly a more archaic time, it also had its advantages of adventure and danger as well.

Being with Fiona intimately is terrific. An adventure in itself. Her appetite for me, for the pleasure I bring her, only brings me closer to her. Our bond now impenetrable, I sense her in ways even I did not realize possible. If it were up to me, she'd stop working for her father, and be my consort all the time. Yes, an old-fashioned way of thinking, but I am already working out a plan to convince her to marry me. Damen and Lydia make it work, and their happiness, their seeming content with the time they have together is what I desire with Fiona.

I know she's a progressive mortal and has made it very clear that being kept by me does not suit her, and since her happiness is paramount to me, she shall have her way.

"Must you go to work today?" I ask her as I lie in bed watching her dress.

"Yes, I must." She turns to face me, buttoning up a new blouse I bought her.

"You know, you don't have to work. You could just stay here with me." My eyes shift between her breasts where her cross dangles. I do wish that she'd take it off, but I understand that it is symbolic of her independence, which I both admire and respect. She has no desire to be controlled, and she proves that she wishes to be with me every day.

"I do have to work, Roman. We've talked about this a million times. I can't just sit around doing nothing, not contributing. That's just not who I am."

"We don't have to sit around. We can travel the world."

She smiles thoughtfully and saunters to the side of the bed, taking a seat. "As wonderful as that sounds, and I do want to travel with you, Roman, my work here isn't finished. And neither is yours. Once you open the casino, then we can go on a vacation to celebrate."

I muse, as she still hasn't realized the magnitude of what we could do, how we could live our lives together. Her human mind cannot yet comprehend our lack of need for casinos, for jobs, her trust fund, for any of it. The work that I've done over the years would take care of her in any fashion she wished for the rest of her life. The only reason that I want to set up the casino as an ongoing funding source for the orphanage is so that when I decide to leave

Las Vegas for another new adventure, that legacy will live on, sustaining itself.

"Vacation, eh?" I ask.

She leans in to kiss me. I don't remember a desire for human food or the tastes it offers, but I imagine that her kisses taste like the sweetest desserts made by the most excellent pastry chefs in all of France. I should take her to France; I think that she'd enjoy the shopping, the cafes, and the romance of it all.

"Yes, vacation. It's what normal people do. Besides, I'm going to talk to my father today about some things."

My romantic desire to sweep my love off to France has been replaced with disdain and anger. "What are you going to talk to him about exactly?" She doesn't have to tell me what she's doing, and she does work for him, but they've avoided any real conversation since the incident at her house.

"Put the fangs away, babe. I think it's a good thing." She gets up and walks to the dressing table to finish getting ready.

In a flash, I'm at her side, angry. "What are you planning to discuss, Fiona?" I ask again, with more fervor, my voice low and agitated.

"He is a reasonable man, Roman. I believe if I sit down and have a frank chat with him about the good your casino will do for the community, and how in turn, granting the permit would make him look good, he will come to see it is the right thing to do. Approve your license."

Humans concern themselves with trying to reason with each other far too much. This is a terrible idea, and I hope from my expression that she can see I'm displeased. To maintain composure, I merely ask, "Do you really think that's such a good idea? It hasn't been that long since..." I don't need to finish my sentence.

Crossing her arms and facing me sternly she replies. "Look, Roman, he's still my dad. He's not the greatest man of all time. He's got some skeletons in his closet that he knows I could expose. I'm not doing this for you, I'm doing it for the children. And he's my father, you can't tell me what to do, so don't even bother trying." She raises her hand to her cross and fidgets with it uncomfortably.

It distresses me to make her feel bad about her relationship with her father, but I have seen how humans like him behave over the last five centuries, and it's not right. They'll betray and forsake their own blood for money and power, and my instincts tell me that he's no different.

"I wouldn't dream of telling you what to do, but may I give you my opinion?" I never need to demand of her, and she gives me her full attention, with less defensive posturing.

"Of course you can, I'm sorry," she says.

"I know that he is your father, but we do agree that he has a rather unsavory character. Would that be a fair assessment?"

"Yes, that would be fair." She rolls her eyes, awaiting the rest.

"Then perhaps this isn't the best time. It's too soon, and you've not reconciled your personal differences just yet. Before you go threatening to uncover all of his dirty deeds, maybe you should consider getting back into his good graces instead? Then, once you're on more cordial terms, you start asking for favors and understanding?" Literally the most diplomatic thing that's ever fallen from my lips. What I wanted to say was fuck this guy, I don't need his license or his casino. I can fund the orphanage on my own, or I could compel a human to get the license for me if that's what I wanted. What I don't fucking want, is her father meddling in our lives. But I stay prudent and gracious.

She looks at me thoughtfully again, scanning my face for a sign of some kind. "While I don't disagree with your strategy overall, I think with my father direct and brutal is the way to go."

I'd love to be brutal with him. I'll not soon be over the almost staking.

"I will never tell you what to do, and I'll support you in any way that I can. Perhaps I should go with you."

"You most certainly should not!" she exclaims.

"Why not? What if you need my protection?"

"I will not need protection. My dad is a conniving asshole, but he's not going to do anything that requires any sort of protection. So you just stand down, vampire. We don't need another scene. I have this under control."

"As you wish, Fiona," I reply. I lean down to kiss her, pulling her into my arms. She smells like fresh linen that's been out in the sun to dry. Clean, and pristine, I want to drag her back to bed and soil the sheets again, just like we did the night before. I deepen our kiss, hoping to lure her back into my bed, and at first, she seems to concede. She then breaks away, giving me one more small kiss before she gathers the things she needs for her day.

"Lana was hoping we could all get together for a late dinner. Are you free tonight?" she asks, hopefully.

"For you, I am always free," I reply, garnering a sweet smile from her. I don't particularly enjoy going out to dinner, other than for the fact that I want her to be healthy and fed. I've been considering hiring a personal chef so that she has food whenever she wants here. I wouldn't know how to make anything, nor do I want to bother learning a skill that will serve no purpose at the end of her life.

My thoughts turn to the end of her life. She is young, and if she marries me, we will have many years together. But not an eternity. Wasting time like she is today frustrates me. We should be enjoying our limited time together. Not pandering to a man who wants me and my whole kind dead.

*A*ll day, I waited for my father to come into his office. Each time I stopped by, the sickeningly sweet secretary placated me with canned responses. He's in a meeting. He's at lunch. He's at an appointment. Never mind the fact, he didn't call me once he found out I came into his office, which is so unlike him. If he's trying to send a message, it's being received loud and clear.

I angle my neck, turning my head left and right, checking to see if Roman's teeth marks can be spotted through the tattoo cover-up cream I bought the other day. So far, I've been able to keep the bruising hidden, which has allowed me to keep my relationship with Roman a secret. It's not that I want to hide him, but until I can get my father to understand, it's the only way to survive right now.

Roman's right, the incident with him and dad is likely still fresh in my father's mind, but I'm going to reassure him he has nothing to fear when it comes to my vampire. Although I won't be able to use those exact words, in my mind, it's what I'll say because when it comes right down to it, Roman's mine.

I've never been a possessive girlfriend until now. Honestly, I'm not sure if I am controlling when it comes to Roman or if it's the bond between us doing some underlying mysticism crap. As much as I didn't want to believe in the vampire/human bond thing, there's no denying it. When Roman is near, I can sense his need, not only to consume my life force to quench his hunger but also his desire to fuck me. I don't know if he realizes this, but he lets off a pheromone so intense when he's thinking about me, it makes my blood dance. The energy I feel, detecting his presence is something I've never felt before. At first, I didn't like it. The sensation was odd and uncomfortable as if I had taken speed and was reaching my peak. My skin prickled and my heart raced, and it scared me. After a few times with Roman, I figured it out. It's the bond, working in some mysteriously magical way and now I find it soothing, relaxing and dare say, exciting. Mostly because I know what's coming.

Finding the tattoo concealer was like hitting the lottery. It was like happenstance when Lana and I were out shopping, and we passed by a parlor. She mentioned getting a tattoo and grabbed me by the arm to pull me inside to inquire about the process. The woman behind the counter was a vampire and laughed at our ridiculous attire, scarves around our necks in hundred degree plus weather. She handed me a tube of cream and a mirror, speaking the unspoken language between women, alive and dead, makeup. Lana and I quickly went to work on our bite marks, completely taken aback by the cream and how it adequately covered the evidence of my lover biting me in the middle of our lovemaking session. "Let it dry fully." Those were her only instructions.

And now, I find myself happy with the results. No one

will know, and thankfully, it doesn't sweat or rub off. How no one has told the world about this cream, I'll never know. Roman could've saved me a lot of trouble if he had known.

Said trouble comes in the form of Leslie, my once best friend turned enemy in the sense she's trying to get me to convert to her religion and denounce the existence of vampires. Even if I believed in her hokey crap, you can't condemn an entity that the government deems exists. Vampires walk among us, with laws we both have to follow. Unless her church is planning to go on a vampire hunt, there isn't anything they can do about it. The constitution has changed with the evolving times.

Still, I'm desperate to know more about Roman and where he came from. Five hundred years is a long time to be alive and roaming the earth. The jealousy within me wants to know about all the women he's been with and whether they're still alive. Did he turn them? Marry them? I mean, obviously, most must be dead unless they're vampires themselves, and that's one thing Roman hasn't mentioned, vampire/vampire relationships. I've wanted to ask, especially where his friend Selene is concerned, but am afraid of his reaction. He says they're friends, but is that with benefits?

What Roman's done before meeting me shouldn't matter, but it does. If he were human, he'd wonder the same about me. For all I know, he's wondering now or just doesn't care because he can sense how I feel about him.

Love... I'm borderline crazy in love with that man. And yes, he's a man in every sense of the word. Except, he's almost too perfect and yet wholly flawed. I hate that he doesn't show emotion, that I can't read him by his expressions and that when I roll over, I find him staring at me. At first, it was creepy, but now I'm used to it. It's Roman's way of passing an endless amount of time. According to him, he has nothing better to do than to watch me sleep. However, I love that he's caring, tends to my needs and is a real gentleman. He holds me at night like any human man would. Kisses me tenderly, caresses me gently, and makes love to me passionately. Yes, it's tough to fight the fact that I'm falling in love with Roman. Something I know my father will never accept and will disown me over. I've asked myself repeatedly if Roman is worth it. The answer is, yes.

With one last look at my appearance, I leave my apartment and head to my father's. I called earlier and spoke to his wife, telling her how much I've missed her and how we need family time. The conversation about killed me, but I'm doing this for the good of the orphanage and Roman. I believe in his project and want my daddy to do the right thing by granting his license.

Outside, my driver waits in the valet line and has the door open for me as soon as I step out of the revolving door. I remember, when I was a kid, I used to play in those doors while my father was gambling. This one time, the door became stuck and wouldn't budge in either direction. I pushed and pushed, but to no avail. It was hotter than Hades, and I couldn't breathe, nor could anyone understand me due to the loud sounds of Las Vegas. At any given time there's music playing, slot machines chiming, people yelling, sirens, and valets whistling for taxicabs. The bellhop thought I was messing around until I started to pass out, and then everything became serious, and he used a metal stanchion to break the glass. It took me a long time before I ever walked through one again.

"Where to, Ms. Weston?"

"My father's house, please."

The driver heads toward the house I grew up in, leaving

the bright lights of the city quickly behind us. When I chose to go to college in California, my dad was irate and demanded I stay here. It was mostly because he didn't want to be alone and he didn't think it was acceptable for a young woman to be five hours away from her father. He's a firm non-believer in letting your children spread their wings and grow. Thing is, if I hadn't left, he probably wouldn't have met his wife. Not that I'm a fan, but she seems to make him happy, unlike the last one or my mother.

My childhood home is a sprawling mansion, set behind a massive rock wall and large wrought iron gate, which bears too many crosses to count. According to my father, he's had the house blessed, which is meant to keep vampires out. Whether it works or not, has yet to be seen. I don't foresee my dad inviting the undead over to see if they can cross the threshold, although I'm tempted to bring Roman over sometime when my dad isn't home, I'm also afraid that whatever my father has done could hurt the man I'm falling in love with.

The new Mrs. James Weston opens the door and holds her arms out to me. Behind my sunglasses, I roll my eyes and happily play along with the woman who is only a few years older than I am. "Fiona, darling," she says in her old world accent as if she's from someplace other than Vegas.

"Hello, Catherine." She used to be Kate with a K, but when Prince William married Catherine, Kate changed her name to be more regal. Didn't help.

"Your father will be so delighted you're here."

Setting my sunglasses on top of my head, I step into the house I once called home. Every time a new wife moves in, the hallway in the foyer changes. It used to be flowers when my mother lived here, then turned to purple, to white and now it's some pinky cream color combination. "Yes, I can't wait to see Daddy." I wink, knowing how much she hates it when I call my father, daddy. "Speaking of, where is he?"

"In his study."

"Thanks." My heels smack down hard onto the marble floors. I don't bother knocking when I reach the ornate door. It's pointless, really. James Weston is sitting at his desk, with his feet propped up, smoking a cigar. "She'll kill you, you know."

"Fiona, I'm surprised to see you here, considering…"

I sigh heavily. "Daddy, I'm an adult, and you should've called before you came over. What you saw--"

"He was trying to kill you."

Shaking my head, I realize it's futile to argue with him, but I have to try. "He wasn't, and I heard your stance on my relationship with him loud and clear, but I need you to remember, I'm an adult and can be with who I want."

"Over my dead body, Fiona."

"Daddy, you're ridiculous. You don't see me whining about you marrying some harpy who is only a few years older than I am, do you? How do you think that makes me feel?"

My father stands and slams his fists on his desk. "No child of mine will give herself to an abomination. Do I make myself clear?"

I have to do something quickly or Roman's idea, which is brilliant and amazing, will never get noticed. "Yes, Daddy. Can we talk about something else?" Like how I have no intention of obeying your archaic rule?

"Of course, sweetheart." And just like that, my father has gone from Hyde to Jekyll in no time at all.

"I have a proposal for you. It's like nothing you've ever seen before." I set the portfolio down in front of my father, who has sat back down. He opens the cover and starts reading. It took me days to retype Roman's proposal to make it my own. This is the only way I know my father will say yes and give Roman the permit he needs to run the casino. I want Roman to succeed, to help those children and the homeless so much that I'm willing to do whatever I have to to get my father to sign on the dotted line.

I pace the room while my dad continues to read and look over the blueprints. Catherine interrupts us and tells us it's dinner time. "Not now," my dad says, waving at her to leave the room. "Shut the door behind you." Maybe paradise at the Weston house is ending sooner than I think.

After what seems like an eternity, my dad closes the file and rests his hands on top of it. "Where did you get this?"

"It's mine," I say automatically. "I have a silent investor, willing to fully fund the project."

A smile spreads across his lips, turning wider. "Fiona, I'm impressed."

"You should be, it's an amazing project," I speak from the heart, wishing I could give Roman all the credit. "I can't offer you the perks the others can, but I'm your daughter, and I'm hoping that's enough. Will you sign the gaming license?"

"Of course I will. It'll be my honor." My dad stands and pulls me into a hug. Step one is complete, now just to break it, Roman.

21

ROMAN

I can sense something isn't right. I'm trying to read the global newspapers I have delivered to me, and a sense of suffocating begins to take hold in my chest. Not needing air, I know this is foreboding, and I'm reasonably sure I know what's about to happen. In the old days, a few hundred years ago or so, there would have been a signal of some kind. A prophetic cloud forming overhead, darkness during the day, or some other ominous message that was more telling, but today, it's a premonition almost; I know something is about to happen.

Of course, I don't want Fiona to talk to her father about my project, or about us. No good can come of that meeting if there's any honesty whatsoever. Some humans cannot be rationalized with, and in my experience, it's best to leave things alone with them. I'm confident in my belief that he cannot be swayed, just as I cannot be something that I am not. I can feel Fiona's apprehension, her nervousness, and it troubles me. But that's not what's happening now. Something's amiss in the underground. Just as I pull my phone from my pocket, it vibrates with an incoming message from Selene.

They're coming. Get to Clutch. Now. No Humans.

They're coming. "They" being the Sisters. The Fates. The ones who both created, and rule us. It's never good when the Sisters come. I've yet to experience it myself until now, and the apprehension is working its way to my core. I type a quick reply indicating that I'm on my way, and leave immediately.

Upon my arrival at Clutch, the neon lights are off, and there's a short line of vampires waiting to get in. Everyone needs to check in when the Sisters arrive, which is protocol. It's somewhat old-fashioned, and you'd think they'd adapt to technology in some way, but there's a master list of the vampires on paper, parchment paper, in fact, getting checked in one at a time. It's as if we're disembarking from the lifeboats that made it off the Titanic. The anxious faces, the furrowed brows, all indicating that a visit from the Sisters was not a treat.

To the chagrin of my kinfolk standing in line, I approach Corban at his usual spot in front of the door, but with much less glee in his eyes. "Brother, any word on why we are being visited?"

"No, mate. No word yet."

"Have you ever been called to a Meeting before?"

Corban shakes his head.

"No, me neither," I add. "It could be nothing." Too bad I don't believe my own words. Personally, I've never had to check in with the Fates before, and honestly never hoped I would have to. I feel like I have nothing to worry about, yet for some reason, I'm worried.

"Maybe, brother. Go on inside, I'll mark you off the list." He waved me past the line and made a check mark next to my name on his clipboard. Fucking paper. Utterly absurd, is all I can think. Clutch is full of faces I've never seen before. The Las Vegas population of vampires has tripled in a short amount of time, and I'm not sure I like it. Not all of us live by the rules, and honestly having these unknowns in town doesn't sit well with me.

Being here is unsettling. I don't like bumping shoulders with the unknowns. I seek out Selene, hoping she can enlighten me as to what's going on. Clutch was chosen for a reason, and like the others around me, I want to know why.

"You didn't try to bring that human of yours, did you?" she hisses from behind me. I turn around and immediately wish I hadn't. Her long dark hair is pulled back into a sleek ponytail, revealing her perfect features, and her angry expression. I've seen Selene angry before, but nothing like this. Her usually soft eyes are stone cold black, and her fangs are visible. A sure sign she's about to attack.

"No, I didn't. And what are you so pissed off about?"

"Do you know how the Sisters notify you that they are coming?" she asks me.

"I don't." It's not something I've been privy to in my life. When the Sisters want to talk to you, they do it their way.

"None of us do. It's fucking terrible, Roman." She pulls a chair out from another vampire and sits down, looking exasperated. If she were human, she'd have a drink in her hand.

"What happened?"

"They take over your mind. They can get right into your fucking head." She looks around as if they might be listening before she continues. "I was sitting at my desk in the back office when suddenly I couldn't move or think on my own. Their voices were soft at first and then firm and rather frightening."

I can't believe this is how the Sisters contact us, going straight to your mind. That's just as unnerving as I suspected her answer would be. "So, what did they say?"

"First it was Clotho. She was as charming as the day we met. She said that she wants to visit her children and that I needed to send word to my local brethren that she's coming. I must have given off the sense of fear, because she sort of consoled me, or rather tried to be soothing." Selene appears paler to me than usual, which is undoubtedly a figment of my own imagination, that isn't even possible. But her hushed tone, coupled with her darting eyes as if she's being watched is troubling at best.

"Selene, we haven't ever been visited by them. What else did they say?" I try to be patient with my friend, but I'm anxious.

"Atropos and Lachesis began to speak. Their tone was far less paternal, and more... stern. Atropos has a shrill voice, and she reminded me that she made me and that I was to do as instructed. I wasn't able to speak at all; I was frozen in place. I could feel myself nodding my head in agreement. I mean I'd never challenge them, nor did I want to, but I was completely unable to give any verbal indication at all. Then Lachesis, who had a kind and soft voice similar to Clotho, said that she and her sisters would be arriving soon, and asked me if I understood my instructions. It was only then that I was able to utter a word. Once I said yes, I understand, my mind and body were released, and it was as if they were never there. Everything around me had gone back to normal."

"So they never said why they were visiting or what they wanted?"

"I told you everything, Roman. That was it."

While I've got nothing to hide, I'm also not sure why

we've all been summoned to check in, which leaves me concerned. Also, the fact that the Sisters chose Selene to be the messenger weighs upon me. "Do you know why they chose to give their message to you? Has anything like this ever happened before?"

"Roman, we've been friends for hundreds of years. Don't you think I'd tell you?" she asks tersely.

"I do. I'm just concerned that you have been selected as some kind of messenger, and I'm trying to discern what the fuck it means. We've been happily flying under the radar for years."

Leaning back in her chair, she looks at me thoughtfully. "I don't know, Roman, but it can't be good. They did say no humans were to be here. I left that part out, but I did tell you, obviously." She anxiously glances around before leaning close to me. "Hopefully they aren't planning to starve us all to death."

Keeping the humans away from the visitation could mean a lot of different things. Our history isn't completely secret, or how we're made. Some humans know, but most are inclined to pretend we don't exist, and there are only a few history books that actually have it right. Unlike how to make bombs or the perfect cake, there's no recipe for how to make a vampire on the Internet or anything like that. We've always tried to keep that as vague as possible.

"I don't think they would do that. We're their children. They, our mothers. There has to be a disruption somewhere that requires a check in, though. It's probably no big deal," I lie. It's a huge deal. I do not know of any situation where the Sisters have visited, and vampires didn't die or weren't punished in some way. Our rules are quite clear, and when we become vampires, we swear an oath to abide by them. In my estimation, someone has done something against the

Covenant and will be made an example of in the very near future.

"You didn't tell your human what's going on, did you?" Selene asks me dryly.

"No, I did not. You summoned me, and I came."

"If you care for her, you should keep it that way. She's a stubborn one. You do not want her showing up here looking for answers while the Sisters are here." Selene doesn't much care for my relationship with Fiona. While she supports my decision and my feelings as my friend, it is clear that she doesn't understand it. Sometimes I don't understand it either.

I nod and reply. "I don't want Fiona anywhere near this place, or this situation until we know why they're here. We've got enough problems with her father."

"Did something else happen?" Selene appears shaken again. "You know that could be why they're coming!"

"That's ridiculous. He's one gluttonous, psycho millionaire human who actually tried to kill me, remember? I didn't do anything."

"You ravaged his daughter."

"She's a willing participant in our relationship. She's never been compelled. She still wears that ridiculous cross, in fact."

"Well, it's possible that almost being staked by her dad is worth a look into down here in Las Vegas, my friend. So prepare yourself for the inquisition should it happen," she said.

I don't want to admit that Selene could be right. Pride is not an emotion that disappears with vampirism, and the fact that I could be made an example of in some way stirs inside me.

"I'm sure one of these degenerates have done something

to violate the Covenant, and we're all just here to witness his punishment. Relax." I need to take my own advice, but now that we've said it, she's quite possibly right.

It's mid-afternoon the day that Fiona is to talk to her father against my wishes, and I'm now trapped inside of a vampire nightclub awaiting my creators' visit. I feel my phone vibrate in my pocket, so I pull it out and turn it off. I cannot sense any bad feeling or danger with her, and I need to stay focused on the impending visit now. I can, however, detect that her agitation has left, and she is calm, and that has to be good enough for now. Mind reading or telekinesis, or telepathy of some kind would have been a way better gift from the Fates, but I need to make do with knowing that she is safe.

If vampires had hearts, mine would be beating through my chest, but instead, I sit stoically, simply waiting.

22

FIONA

*M*y driver pulls away from my father's house. The smile on my face says it all. My pitch was on point, and my dad loved it. I have never seen him grin from ear to ear before, at least not when talking business with me. I felt a sense of pride when he patted me on the back. It took everything in me to keep the secret, knowing if I exposed the project as Roman's, my father would've ripped everything up and kicked me out. Mostly, I want my father to see me as someone who knows the business. That's where this project with Roman comes in.

I want to work with Roman, as his partner. I know it's not what he wants, but after seeing the orphanage and reading his proposal, this is something I can get behind one-hundred percent. I want to use my degree and do something meaningful instead of being my father's lackey. My dad pays me to entertain the investors while sorting through the garbage they present, and the only thing he really cares about is who is padding his pockets. Out of every proposal I've seen, nothing compares to what Roman has put together. He deserves this opportunity, and I'm going to make it happen for him.

Although, I fear what I've done might upset Roman. I have to make sure I lay it all out there for Roman and let him know that everything I've done is for him and his project.

Halfway home, I call him. The phone rings once and goes to voicemail, which means Roman's busy. He's done this before when he's in a meeting, so I send a text, telling him how the meeting went with my father. I leave out the details about lunch, knowing the consumption of food doesn't really mean anything to him, though he does show great concern for my dietary habits. Honestly, my eating must be a complete bore for him. Maybe it's something I need to do when we're not together, so he's not feeling awkward. However, that would severely limit our dates, and I really like going out with Roman.

As soon as I get home, I check for any new messages and am saddened to find none. Roman barely lets me wait longer than twenty minutes without returning at least my text. I try him again, and this time his phone doesn't even ring. I leave him a message, hoping he can grasp the desperation in my voice. Standing outside, dark clouds loom overhead. From this high up, the people down on the street look like ants, seeking shelter from the impending rain. I glance at my weather app; nothing but sun for the next fifteen days.

I suppose it's not odd for a freak storm to hit, but usually, we get alerts, letting us know what's coming. With my phone in my hand, I call Roman again. I know I'm bordering on crazy girlfriend status, but I have news I want to share. And he was worried about me going over to my father's considering what happened in my apartment not too long ago, so why isn't Roman answering?

As the night goes on, I continue to stand on my balcony, saying Roman's name repeatedly. I don't need to yell because I know he can hear me. Up until I left my father's house, I felt our bond. All through telling my dad about Roman's plan, our bond was giving me the confidence I needed to get through the meeting without unleashing on my father for his archaic views. Yet, all of a sudden, I feel cold and weak, almost like energy Roman and I share is no longer flowing.

I finally give in to my tears when my next call goes right to voicemail. The sound of his voice, telling me he can't come to the phone right now as if he's talking directly to me is too much to handle. I hang up, already having left multiple messages.

"Roman, where are you?" I say out into the open, hoping for an answer, waiting for him to knock on my door any second. "I know you can hear me, and I'm worried. Please come home." I sob, and slide down the wall, the rough concrete scraping my knees as I do. This pain is nothing compared to what my heart is feeling.

I don't know how long I stay outside, waiting to hear from Roman. When I look down at my phone, it's dead, which sends a rush of panic through me. I scramble into my home and plug in the device, praying there's a missed call from my vampire. The Apple symbol shines and then changes to my home screen.

Nothing.

Not a single notification.

Something must've happened to Roman, and he's hurt, it's the only logical explanation. I mean, it's unlikely, unless he's run into someone deranged like my father. If Roman was to be staked, is there a body or does he turn to dust? How would I know? It's not like he carries a call my consort card in his wallet in the case of death. Thinking Roman could be dead makes me physically ill. I rush to the bathroom and expel the contents of my lunch into the toilet. I can't lose him, not without a chance to say goodbye.

I clean up, washing my face and brushing my teeth. I avoid looking at myself in the mirror mostly of fear I'll start crying again when I see my reflection. I have no doubt my eyes are bloodshot, my cheeks are red, and I probably have snot dried on my face.

Back in my living room, I start to pace again, stopping only to look at my phone to see if Roman has reached out. He's never waited this long to return one of my calls. It's useless for me to look.

There's really only one person I can ask, and that's Lydia. She's my resident expert on all things vampire, and maybe she can shed some light on why mine would suddenly disappear on me. Unfortunately, this requires me to leave, which means I need to fix my hair and make-up.

After I reapply most of my make-up, I change quickly and head toward the Bellagio, hoping Lydia's working. It would've made sense for us to exchange numbers, but during our double date, I was so in tuned to Roman, I didn't give Lydia and Damen a second thought. I just wanted to be with him, and I completely ignored everyone around me.

The clouds from earlier cast dark shadows over the grand marquees that generally light the path of the Strip. It's an eerie feeling out on the street tonight. People are quiet, almost somber like something terrible has happened. As I cross the road, I pull my phone out of my purse and look at my notifications. There's nothing. I barely have a signal, which I find odd.

At the Bellagio, I rush through the lobby and stand impatiently at the hostess stand. When she finally rounds the corner, I smile. "Hi, yes, can you tell me if Lydia's working tonight?"

"She is. Would you like to sit in her section?" Yes and no. What I really want to do is talk to her, but I don't want to get stuck ordering food I'm not going to eat. "Can you tell her Fiona Weston is here?" The hostess nods and disappears. Once again, I find myself pacing and checking my phone as I do. Too many hours have passed since I've heard from -Roman and with the way the weather is tonight, I really don't want to be alone.

"Hi, Fiona," Lydia says as she approaches.

"Is there somewhere we can go to talk? It'll only take a minute or so." Lydia nods and points to the wall, across the hall.

"What's going on?"

"It's Roman."

"What about him?" she asks.

My hands wring together as I try to compose my words. "I'm trying not to be a crazy girlfriend, but you have to understand since I've met Roman he hasn't left me alone until today. Earlier this morning when I left him to go see my father, Roman begged me not to go because he and my dad do not get along, but I went, and I promised him I'd call as soon as I was done. I did, but Roman's not returning my calls, and I'm having trouble feeling our bond."

"I haven't seen Roman, but I imagine he's at Clutch."

"Why would he be there?"

She leans in closer. "Have you seen any vampires around today?" I look over her shoulder and glance at the people walking by. None of them carries the mark.

"No, why is that?"

"The Sisters are here. Every vampire has to report to the Keeper."

"The Keeper? I have no idea what you're talking about, Lydia."

"The Keeper is a vampire chosen by the Fates to deliver the message of their impending arrival. I don't know who the Keeper is, as Damen didn't say, but I do know, they're in a meeting."

"Wait, who are the Sisters?"

"The vampires' creators. According to Damen, they only come when times are dire, or someone has broken one of the Covenants."

Roman and I haven't discussed his laws. I hadn't really asked either. Deep down I figured they were like our Ten Commandments; thou shalt not kill being the most important.

"What if they're here because of me?

Lydia looks at me oddly and takes a step back.

"My dad tried to kill Roman, and Roman attacked my dad."

Her eyes go wide, and her mouth drops open. What I thought to be a skirmish, could possibly be a punishment for Roman.

23

ROMAN

*M*inutes turn into hours as the crowd inside Clutch grows. It seems that vampires from all over Las Vegas and the surrounding areas have been instructed to congregate here, and not unlike humans, the rumors and speculation are at an all-time high. Hushed voices around the room take guesses at what brings the Sisters to town. From what we know, essentially from hearsay or folklore, they visit a Clutch vampire club only to bring down punishment upon those who have disobeyed, or broken a sacred Covenant.

There are no humans permitted during this time, and some of the vampires look like they should have fed before coming here. Technology hasn't mastered any sort of synthetic blood substitute like you might see in movies or television, and there has been no need for us to store blood for centuries. Humans willingly provide it to us these days, but for those who arrived hungrily, they'll be in misery if we're stuck here for an extended period of time.

Since it appears that we had notice, I suppose I could have notified Fiona I would be detained for an unknown amount of time, but that wouldn't have been sufficient. She asks a lot of questions, and while I love her inquisitive nature, the lack of answers I am able to provide in this particular situation would have caused her more distress than ignoring her call and turning off my phone. I can't help it, I'm agitated. I want to know what happened with her father today, and I want my freedom. Being trapped in the bar without the ability to leave has me feeling like a caged animal.

Each of us met the Sisters at least one time. On the day of our rebirth. The thing about that day is that no vampire remembers it. I don't recall their faces or voices. I don't even know if I met all three at one time, or if I was passed around, or even what I said to become a vampire. I have a vague recollection of a world before I was a vampire, and photographic memory of every moment after becoming a vampire. That sliver of time in the middle, actually becoming a vampire? Don't remember a bit of it. None of us do. It's either the most wonderful feeling in the world, or it's the worst, and that is why it's blocked out. Although the Sisters are known for having a purpose to every single thing that they do, so it's probably intentional.

Selene looks more agitated than ever, and she leans across the bar where we've settled ourselves in to wait. "Do you remember what drinking tasted like? Or how it made you feel?" she asked me randomly.

As I think back over the years of my life, I can't say that I do. "No, I suppose I wasn't much of a drinker before." I surmise this with no reasonable evidence to support my guess.

"Do you remember much of your life before?"

"Selene, why are you asking me all of these questions? Are you okay?" I grow concerned for her well being after unexpectedly becoming the Keeper. We all knew that a Keeper existed, but I personally presumed that someone held that role and was aware of their responsibility. I had no idea that the chosen vampire would be overtaken by the Sisters whenever they saw fit.

"I'm fine, Roman. I'm just thinking about life before. Would it have been easier to be a foolish and infantile human? Would it have been better?" A wistful look passes over her face before she shakes her head as if jolting lose the thought.

"I don't think it would have been any easier. It would have been different. And not nearly as interesting a life. But it doesn't matter; we're not human, Selene. We haven't been human for over five hundred years. We have experienced the human condition time and time again and survived long beyond their trials and tribulations, and we shall continue to do so for another five hundred years or more." I'm not entirely satisfied I believe my own monologue, but Selene looks disturbed by the events unfolding, and I do care for her.

Smiling, she lets out a light laugh. "Maybe you're right. I don't like all this waiting. It agitates me. Disrupts my business, too." She glances around the room at all the vampires with nothing to buy; all the lost revenue without any humans was evidently on her mind as well.

"Hopefully it'll happen soon. Whatever it is. I have shit to do too."

"Like your human?" she teases me.

"Yes. Exactly. Like my human." I chuckle.

Just then, the lights flicker, and the vampires milling about all become silent. It's happening. The Sisters, the Fates as they are, have arrived. I'm not sure what I expected; a plume of magic smoke and they'd appear, but that's not what happened at all. They walk in through the front door, the crowd parting before them as they approach the center of the room. Almost floating, they each had a familiar look to me, as if I'd met them before, which of course I had, but I have no exact recollection of it.

The slightest of tight-lipped, sly smiles across each of their lips, the only other thing they have in common with each other is the ethereal gowns they're dressed in. They don't appear to have that "Mistress of the Night" look about them, so that stereotype isn't their fault. In fact, they are quite beautiful, like Greek goddesses. That's what their attire reminds me of. Still, no one has spoken, but everyone in the room is standing, staring and waiting.

"My children," the first one said. Her wispy blonde hair falls in waves around her face and down her back. "I am Clotho. You do not remember me, but you have all met me, as your former selves. As a useless bag of blood and bones before you became my children." Her voice is soft and kind, almost soothing. "My sisters and I are here because someone has broken the rules of the Covenant. Our sacred and binding Covenant." Her kind face turns into a scowl, and her perfect white teeth draw out past her pale pink lips.

All I can think is that it wasn't me, so who's the asshole? Selene and I make eye contact, giving a knowing glance and then we're both scanning the room as Clotho begins to roam the room as if she's floating. The other sisters, Atropos and Lachesis, have not identified themselves yet, and they stand to watch their sister as she examines the faces around her. There have to be two or three hundred vampires in the room, maybe more, and she's stopping to make eye contact with each of them.

I now wish that I'd blended myself into the crowd, and didn't have a front row seat for what was about to happen.

Flying under the radar has been my specialty for years, and emerging as anything other than ordinary and obedient is not what I want. Fortunately for me, Clotho stops in front of a vampire I've never seen before. The immediate fear in his eyes as if he's been picked out is evident. The human tendency to fight or flee is less in a vampire, particularly with human interaction; however, I'm quite sure from the near quiver in this vampire's lip that he knows he's in trouble.

"Egan. My child. Step forward." She lifts her hand, gesturing to him.

Reluctantly, the vampire does as she asks.

"Come." She turns back toward where her sisters are still standing, and now grinning.

Egan follows her to the center of the room, then drops to his knees. "Clotho! Please take mercy on me!" he begs. From what I can gather, no one in the room but the Sisters knows what his violations are.

It is then that the Sister with black hair, similar to her blonde sister, long and wavy down her back speaks. She is not as kind, or as demure. "Shut up, you pig!" She sneers.

Egan does as he's told as we all watch the third sister, the one with auburn hair, approach him without menace. She walks around him, gently resting her hand on the top of his head as she circles. "Egan," she says almost tauntingly. "Do you know what you've done?" As Egan opens his mouth to reply, she takes a fistful of his hair roughly, lowering her face to his. "I suggest that you be honest. It will make this much easier for you."

"Yes," Egan whispers.

"Tell your brethren what you've done to make us come here to administer punishment!" She releases him violently, causing him to fall back to the ground.

"I have not followed the rules of the Covenant," he says, head hanging low. What fucking rule could he have broken?

"Which of the rules have you taken upon yourself to disregard? Rules that are set up to protect our kind. Rules that keep us safe among the mortals, and give us the ability to roam freely in their world. What did you do?!" she demands, appearing to lose patience.

"I have compelled humans wearing the cross."

The Sister with the black hair laughs, but it's more of a deranged cackle. "Do you honestly think that we would come here because you compelled a few humans? Egan! Confess! Now!" she demands, her impatience becoming evident.

As if he were taking a sigh, he pauses before answering. "I compelled humans who did not wish to be compelled. And then I fed on them."

"And what happened when you greedily fed on these humans, Egan?" Clotho's soft voice inquires.

"I drained them. I couldn't stop myself. I was so hungry, and they were so beautiful." He looks up at the Sisters, now all in a line before him, looking down upon him.

"Oh, my child. You knew the rules regarding this behavior. It's not acceptable and puts our kind at great risk. You must pay for these sins," Clotho says sympathetically as she takes a step backward.

"Please have mercy on me," Egan begs, knowing that it's too late. He killed humans. And not just one, several it seems. For pleasure, and for no other reason.

The red-haired Sister steps forward. "Egan, you are now sentenced to defanging, followed by death. Your crimes are egregious, and there is no retribution befitting such a break in the Covenant. You've endangered your brothers and sisters, and therefore your life must be taken."

She steps behind Egan, grabbing him by the hair, and pulling his head back, exposing his neck dramatically as the dark-haired sister approaches. "Lachesis, hold him still as I take his fangs." She grins manically; she enjoys this, which somewhat appalls me.

"Yes, Atropos."

Now I know who is who, and it's pretty clear that Atropos is the punisher in this trio. While I try not to give off any red flags of my own, I watch in horror as she pulls out Egan's fangs – by hand. I've never seen anything like it in my life. If a vampire sustains a nonfatal injury, the parts injured will regenerate. It's a perk of being immortal. I imagine that if there weren't more to this punishment, his fangs would grow back, but by the amount of screaming that has begun, it must be painful as fuck.

The rest of the room remains silent as Clothos approaches with a long, medieval sword and hands it to Atropos. Egan is on his knees, crying if such a thing exists for a vampire. I've not witnessed a vampire experience pain such as this, so I'm not even clear what the fuck is happening until Atropos wields the sword well above her head, and with one massive swing decapitates Egan.

Never having witnessed a vampire beheading or a vampire death for that matter, the grey sticky substance that spewed from his corpse was not only shocking, but it also sprayed bits of his insides on anyone standing nearby, including myself. As I look down at the muck that has splattered on my shirt and jacket, I realize that Egan's head has rolled next to my foot and I look back up at the Sisters, who all have grins on their faces.

"Now that we've taken care of that, one of your sisters has not checked in. We will be leaving to address that violation, and we will be returning afterward," Clotho says without any emotion, just her soft and kind voice.

Atropos catches my glance. "You. Roman," she says without inflection.

"Yes?" I reply.

"Burn his body. And you, Keeper!" she yells at Selene.

"Yes, Sister?" Selene replies.

"Make sure it's taken care of. We will know."

"Yes, Sister."

With sword in hand, Atropos walks to the front door, Sisters in tow. In a moment, they are gone, and I'm standing in a room full of stunned vampires with a severed head, a body and a set of fangs to dispose of. What the fuck?

24

FIONA

"*S*ay something, Lydia. Do you think Roman's in trouble?"

"I don't know, Fiona. I wish I could help, but my hands are tied. I can't betray Damen."

"But you're married to a vampire. Doesn't that give you special privileges or something?"

Lydia shakes her head and glances toward the restaurant. I'm keeping her from her job, which is selfish, but I need answers. "Being married to a vampire means I have a husband who is going to outlive me and likely die from starvation after I pass. The bond Damen and I have is nothing like the one you're sharing with Roman. It goes beyond deep. It's eternal. But it doesn't mean I'm privy to vampire business nor am I allowed to insert myself. When Damen received the text today, he kissed me, told me the Sisters were coming and that he'd see me later."

"How could he be so confident?" I ask, hoping Roman is feeling the same way.

"Because Damen hasn't done anything wrong. The life Damen and I have is simple. We both work, and when we're not working, we're together. In fact, some might say we're boring, choosing to sit in front of the television rather than hit a nightclub."

"So you don't go to Clutch?"

Lydia shrugs. "Sometimes. Damen and I will go on dates. We like to dance and there he can be free to be himself without judgment."

"Lydia?" We both turn at the sound of her name being called by the hostess. "You have a table waiting for their check." She doesn't wait for Lydia to respond before walking back into the restaurant.

"I have to get back to work." Lydia starts to walk away, but I grab onto her arm. I don't know what to do or where to go. Going back to my apartment seems logical, but I don't know if Roman will go there when he's done with his vampire business or not, and I don't have a key to his place.

"What am I supposed to do?" My voice breaks. I'm on the verge of hitting the wall of emotions. I want to cry because my heart is breaking, thinking Roman's in trouble because of my father. If I find out my dad alerted someone, I'll never forgive him.

If I'm expecting Lydia to placate me, I'm sorely mistaken. She removes my hand from her arm and steps back. "Look, you seem really nice, and Roman seems to really like you, but I can't help you. Vampires have a Covenant they must follow, and you have to respect that and know Roman's going to keep secrets from you. He has to. Accepting Roman for who he is, comes with accepting the good, the bad and the secrets. Damen can't always tell me everything, and I respect that." Lydia walks back into the restaurant without a glance, while I'm left standing in the middle of the vast hallway with people bustling by, bumping into me as if they don't see me.

After being hit one too many times by fleeing tourists, I finally start moving toward the exit. Lucky for me, I only live a few blocks from this hotel, and the walk is easy. As soon as I step outside, I notice the lack of people, which is odd for Las Vegas. Sure, during the holidays we have fewer tourists, but not in the middle of the summer. Also, it's cold, much colder than I remember it being when I arrived at the Bellagio.

My arms cross, and I rub them up and down against my skin to create some friction as I walk down the sidewalk to the street. There isn't anyone milling around for the fountains either, which never happens, and the lights are dimmer now than they were before I arrived. People pass by in a rush to get wherever they need to be. I pick up on bits and pieces of their conversations, hearing things about an energy surge, the end of the world is happening and the UFOs have finally left Area 51. Unfortunately, all three are more likely to occur in Nevada. We always have those waiting to be abducted by aliens or predicting the world is going to end. However, Las Vegas does consume the most energy, and a surge is likely.

By the time I get home, the streetlights are out, and police officers are trying to direct traffic by flashlight, telling drivers to return to their homes and stay there. The automatic door for my hotel is out of order, and inside, none of the slot machines are working. There's a line at the elevator, and while tempted to wait, something tells me it's not safe. The last thing I want to do is get stuck inside a cramped car, with no oxygen. I'd have an instant panic attack. I make my way toward the stairs, but the door won't budge. "What the hell?"

"It's on a timer," one of the security guards says. "And we can't access it because the computer went down."

"What's going on?"

He shakes his head. "Don't know, but we're short staffed, and people are starting to freak out. If the power doesn't return soon, I fear we're going to have a riot on our hands."

I have a feeling he's right. When people tend to panic, violence manages to take over. It's the trickle effect. One person throws a rock and all of a sudden, the next person thinks it's fun and does the same thing, and so on. "How am I supposed to get upstairs?" I ask the guard.

"Right now, you can't until the fire department arrives to take down the door. Unfortunately, every hotel is experiencing the same thing and --"

"And let me guess, we're on the list?"

He nods and grimaces slightly. "Yes, ma'am."

I sigh heavily, realizing there isn't anything I can do, but wait. "What about food? Drinks?"

"I'm not sure, you'll have to check the restaurants."

I'm tempted to head back to the Bellagio and find Lydia, but I don't want to be caught somewhere and end up stuck. It's best to stay near my home and wait out whatever electrical storm is going on. I find a spot along the wall, but facing the window so I can see what's going on outside even though my vision is clouded by the darker tempered glass. At best, I can see people running, trying to seek shelter from the unknown. I pull out my phone, only to find it dead. Either I didn't charge it enough or whatever is going on outside has messed with our electronics as well. It would make sense.

As time goes on, people become increasingly agitated. Children are restless, people are pacing, and voices are starting to increase. Everyone is on edge. The anxiousness of the people around me turns into anger, which results in a lot of yelling. We want answers or at least some news on what's going on and how long we're going to be without power. There isn't a time I can remember when the entire city was dark. Honestly, this is unheard of and quite odd. I have an eerie feeling this electrical outage has to do with whatever Roman and his friends are up to.

The longer I sit here, the more scared I become. Not only for myself but Roman as well. I need him. Not just to feel safe in his arms but to know he's okay.

25

ROMAN

*A*fter I drag the vampire corpse to the back alley behind Clutch, Selene hands me a bottle of lighter fluid and a fancy lighter. I heave the body into the dumpster against the wall and squirt the pungent smelling accelerant all over it. Igniting the lighter, I toss it on top of the body, just before launching Egan's head in with the rest of him. I run my hands through my hair, watching the fire burn brightly while Selene stands silently next to me.

Neither of us knows what to say. While neither of us was in any kind of trouble ourselves, that visit was dramatic and stressful. There's no other way to describe it. The Sisters have an aura about them that invokes fear, even when you know you have no reason to be concerned. The sky above us had turned a dark purple and gray, and the city seemed to have lost its usual buzzing sound. Typically I'm tuned into the clatter of the humans as they toured, and the ringing of the slot machines; they're much like white noise to me. But what I hear is almost a deafening silence.

"Do you hear that?" I ask Selene, breaking our silence.

"Hear what?" she asks.

"The sound of nothing." I turn my gaze back up to the sky and notice the wind picking up.

Selene also looks up, shaking her head from whatever her thoughts were, and she glances back at me, appearing surprised. "I didn't realize it until you pointed it out. The power is out in the city." She pauses before another revelation hit her. "The humans will surely begin losing their shit at any moment. You know how they panic when they have no control over the elements." My thoughts immediately shift to Fiona. I need to get to her.

"I need to go."

"What if the Sisters come back?" she asks.

"Then text me to come back, but I need to go. I need to make sure Fiona is okay."

Selene rolls her eyes. "That human is going to get you in trouble, Roman. You need to check yourself. I know you think you love her – I can see it in your eyes, so don't even bother trying to deny it. But you are setting yourself up for everlasting heartache if you let this get any deeper. She will die. And you will be alone. Don't you see that?" She is almost pleading with me, but I just don't care. Fiona's lifetime is enough for me to have eternal love. Selene will find hers someday, but you can't explain that, and it's not the time. I need to go.

"Selene, someday you will understand. I promise you. But the Sisters have left, and I need to go. There's no reason to stay for any of us. We were essentially dismissed while they go find the vampire who was foolish enough not to check in."

Pursing her lips, she shrugs her shoulders. "I suppose you're right. But for the love of all that is sacred, be fucking careful. I have a bad feeling about things that I can't shake. I don't like it, and I think you'd be safer with your kind right now."

I appreciate her loyalty and her unwavering friendship. While she may be right, I need to go to Fiona. Leaning in toward her, I pull her in for a hug, her very least favorite human interaction. "Thank you, Selene."

"Ugh, unhand me." She pushes me away with a grin. "You're too human. It's so annoying. Just go." I know she is teasing me, but there's also some truth to it. I've adapted to living an immortal mortal life. A concept foreign to many vampires, I truly live the vast majority of my time outside the supernatural other than for sustenance.

I move less quickly than usual as I go to Fiona's, taking in the scene around me. What appears to be an electrical storm has descended upon the city, but I know it's the Sisters. Clutch didn't experience the power outage that I see all around, and the humans who are out, are scattering like bugs. I can sense their heightened anxiety. As I hone in on Fiona, I can discern her anguish, and I pick up the pace.

As I approach her building, I feel her upset more. Once I'm inside, I find her immediately, lifting her off the floor into my arms.

"Fiona," I whisper into her hair, holding her tightly. Expecting her to be relieved, I'm shocked when she pushes me away.

"What the fuck, Roman?" I can see that she's been crying, but she also looks like she wants to punch me.

"Fiona, I couldn't talk. I'm sorry you're upset, but it's imperative that you stay out of these matters."

"You couldn't have told me that before you took off? I have been worried sick about you! You know that I thought something terrible may have happened!?"

Her concern is evident, and I can see that I should have

sent her a message of some kind assuring her that things would be okay. The monster inside me doesn't always think of these things. "Fiona, we are bonded. You would feel it if something happened to me."

"Are you sure everything is okay? Lydia told me the Sisters have come."

"You went to see Lydia? Fiona, I am sorry that I did not inform you of the visit. It is an unusual circumstance, and it's best to keep you as far removed from them as possible. But know this. You are mine. And I am yours. You need to understand that the life of a vampire can become complicated at times, and you will not always get the answers that you desire. This has to be acceptable to you Fiona, or we will not work." I don't mean for it to sound like an ultimatum because it's not. But, if Fiona cannot respect the Covenant in which I must abide by, she will lead a life of misery and could put us both in danger.

"You need to explain more to me, Roman. I've been wandering the streets looking for you. I need you to communicate with me." I understand her needs, and I want to compromise with her, explain our history and how we became who, or rather what, we are.

I realize that we are still standing in the lobby, and I don't understand why she's not safely upstairs in her home. "Why are you down here? You should be upstairs."

She waves her hand at the building dramatically. "Everything here is run on electric, so the doors and the elevator are locked because there's no power. So, I'm stuck down here."

"Come. We are going to my place." I take her by the hand and pull her behind me.

In light of the storm, and the high anxiety of the city, I make the decision that we will walk the short distance to my place without using supernatural speed. I do not want to draw any undue attention to us, and while I'm pretty sure that the vampires are free to leave Clutch, I don't see any others out and about at the moment. When emotions are running high, it is then, that humans who pretended to be supportive of those unlike them tend to show their true colors, and I've seen first hand how poorly that can end for vampires.

We arrive at my home, where the power is out as well, but we are able to get into the building without issue. When we get inside, I sit Fiona on the couch and cover her with a warm blanket. Her skin is ice cold, almost as cold as mine.

I watch her snuggle into the blanket, and then I settle in next to her. "Fiona, I'm going to explain to you how vampires are created, and who the Sisters are. They made us, and gave us the mark of the Fates as it's referred to."

"Okay," she replies quietly, seeming somewhat uneasy.

I rest my hand on her leg and gently rub it. "I don't want you to be scared, I want you to understand. When I am called away, it is not a choice. It is a requirement that I go, or there will be terrible consequences for my disobedience. I will never leave you for any other reason. Do you understand?"

A tear begins to form in the corner of her eye, and as I reach up to wipe it away, she smiles. "I'm sorry that I lost my shit, Roman. This whole thing is just so new to me. It's moved so fast, and it is overwhelming at times. I was so worried."

I pull her into my arms. "I understand, and that's why I want you to know more about who I am and where I came from," I reply. "I care very deeply about you, Fiona. More so than anyone I've met in five hundred years." I want to tell her I love her, but I can't say it. I'm not sure why, but the timing isn't right. She needs to hear what I have to say first.

"Me too, Roman." She gives me a small smile. "Now tell me about your creators, these Sisters."

"Okay."

I start telling her what I know, from the beginning, which is the luring of a human soul. "Clotho, the blonde goddess, who seems to float with gentility and speak with the softest of voices, compels a human. Basically, she picks her target. I know not what the specifications for her are, other than that most of us appear to have been turned in our early thirties, in human years."

"So, she just goes around picking humans randomly?" Fiona asks.

"Truthfully, I'm not sure," I admit. "No one really knows what makes the Sister pick one human over another. From what we've gathered about ourselves over time, we come from all walks of life. Good people, bad people, boring people, adventurous people; we're all very different." I think back to the many vampires I've met in my travels. There are vampires all over the world, in every city.

"Clotho makes promises of not only immortality but a life of wealth, happiness and a need for nothing. The appeal of a sexy and elite lifestyle draws in most humans, but we weren't given a choice; we were compelled. Only the Sisters can make the determination of who becomes a vampire and who does not. It is then that we agree in exchange for the immortal, we will obey the Covenant for eternity."

"You do lead a sexy life; I have to admit she fulfilled that end of the deal whether you were compelled or not. You certainly weren't duped in that regard," Fiona says dryly.

Letting out a small chuckle, I nod. "Yes, I suppose that is true. But what comes next is most unpleasant. Once we agree, under duress, of course, that we wish to live the immortal life, Atropos appears. Equally beautiful as Clotho, after all, she is a goddess, she takes away our human life."

"What do you mean she takes away your human life? She killed you?"

"Well, close. She drained me of my blood to within an inch of my life. If not for becoming a vampire at that point, any human would die from blood loss alone."

"What the fuck?! She sounds awful!" Fiona pulls the blanket up to her neck, balling herself up beneath it.

"It is not as bad as it sounds," I say to reassure her, although that's not entirely true. The thrill of being bitten, by a goddess, a beautiful, sexual creature is instant and euphoric. Until it's not. It begins as a beautiful bond, a connection to her, but as your human body starts to shut down, lacking what it needs to keep the organs running, it becomes painful and suffocating. The heart slows down, unable to pump blood, as there's not enough to supply the life force of humanity.

Fiona's hanging on every word as I continue to explain the process of how we came to be. "What happens? Is this where you become a vampire, so you don't die?"

"Lachesis, the third sister, then feeds you her blood."

"That's when it happens?"

"Somewhere after that. As a human, drinking the blood of a goddess is surreal, and at the time, all I remembered was being so thirsty. I think that if I truly realized I was drinking the blood of another being, I'm not sure I'd have continued if given a choice."

As the words leave my mouth, I realize I never had a choice. My life is my life now, and I make the most of it. An animal instinct that is bestowed upon us somewhere in this process takes over from time to time, reminding me that I'm not human anymore, I am a savage. I drink the blood of humans for survival, and one day long ago, a day I do not remember, I survived on bread and hunting I'd imagine. I guesstimate this since my human memories were erased. I have no idea what my human name was if I had any loved ones who looked for me or what my human origin is at all.

"Fiona, I am sworn by the rules of the Covenant. It is part of my agreement in being alive at all. They are my masters, and when they summon, I must go. It is never a good omen when the Sisters visit."

"Have you met them over the years? Do they summon you all often?"

"They do not. In fact, they've never summoned any Clutch of vampires who I have been near or around, and I've only heard stories. It is an unpleasant gathering, to say the least."

"I'm so sorry, Roman. I didn't mean to jump to conclusions." She gets up, wrapping the blanket around herself. "Let's get you cleaned up, and then let's go to bed. You've got something all over your shirt."

That's definitely a story for another day.

26

FIONA

*R*oman and I are on our third straight day of staying in his apartment. The only outside contact either of us has had is paying for the delivery guy each time he brought me food. I wish I could say everything was perfect, and for the most part, it has been, except Roman's incessant need to check his phone every few minutes.

"Do you need me to leave?" I ask, the second he picks up his phone.

"No, why?" Roman doesn't look at me but sighs at whatever's on his screen before setting his phone down on the coffee table. I'm tempted to pick it up, but it wouldn't do me any good. I don't know his passcode and wouldn't get very far with it because of his quickness, which is a definite drawback in our relationship.

"I don't know, Roman. You seem to be more focused on your phone than you are on me."

Roman looks at me. He beckons me with his finger, and while I'm tempted to defy him, I don't. I sit, facing him so I can see into his eyes while he tells me what's going on. I know he's on edge with the Sisters being here, but I'm nervous. What if Roman is in trouble?

He leans over and places his lips lightly on my cheek, peppering kisses until he reaches my neck. His tongue darts out and roams over the puncture marks his teeth have left. His hand grips the back of my neck. The force pulls me to him, and he whispers my name against my flesh. As much as I want to give into him, to have him deep inside me, I want answers more, and there's been something plaguing my mind for a while now.

"Roman, stop." I push against him and sit back. I think about standing, but I know Roman will only do the same. I swear, being with a vampire has its perks unless you want to fight with one than you're at a disadvantage.

"I'm sorry, Fiona."

"Don't be sorry, Roman. Just tell me what's so important on your phone that you keep looking at it. Is it Selene?"

"Selene?"

I nod and bite the inside of my cheek. "I have a feeling there's something more between you than you've shared. I know she's your best friend, but after the story, you told me the other day..." I shrug. "I don't know, call it women's intuition or something."

Roman stands, picks up his phone, and walks toward the windows overlooking the city. For the most part, Las Vegas has returned to normal, but it's still overcast and gloomy, which honestly makes me feel depressed. The electricity though seems to function for most of the day. I don't even want to know how much money the city has lost since the arrival of the Sisters.

"She's the first vampire I met after the change occurred."

"Have you been with her? You know, intimately." I hate

myself for asking him this question, but I have to know. If they once shared a bond, she may be a danger to me.

Lightning fast, Roman pulls me from the couch, so I'm standing in front of him. His hand brushes my hair lightly, but the silence between us grows. My heart aches, knowing he's either going to keep his affair with her a secret or never tell me what I need to know. I turn away, unable to look at him.

"It's not what you think, Fiona."

I turn to face him. He looks troubled. "So what's it like?"

"When we are first turned, we have a barrage of emotions running through us. We want to feed, we want to fuck, and we want to kill."

When he says kill, my throat goes dry. As gentle as Roman is, I forget he's a natural born killer and could break me in half with the flick of his wrist. Or take the brutality route and rip me from limb to limb, keeping me alive long enough to watch him murder me. I suppose he could suck my blood until my heart stops beating. It doesn't matter which because I'll never be able to stop him.

"The Sisters... a thousand years ago there was a revolution. Hunters worked tirelessly to destroy the vampire. Back then, my ancestors killed for sport. They drained humans because they felt like it and kept human consorts by the dozen, against their will, sucking their blood whenever they saw fit. The humans banned together and revolted, setting up traps, staking vampires every chance they could. The Sisters were beside themselves. Their children were being murdered, and while some deserved it, not all did.

"The Sisters met with the world leaders to create a pact of sorts where their creations could walk among the humans as long as we were born with our humanely morals and values intact. We wouldn't kill any humans unless they posed a grave threat to us and in exchange, we'd contribute to society. Vampires would walk the earth with a purpose."

"What purpose does a vampire have?"

Roman glances toward the window before looking back at me. "We don't. There's folklore saying the Sisters compelled the leaders into giving them what they wanted. No one will ever be able to prove it because if the Sisters heard about anyone trying to uncover the truth, their life would end. No questions asked."

"How come we never learned about this in school?

"Did you learn about mythology?"

I nod.

He nods as well. "The God of Death is Thanatos, he's the brother of the Sisters."

"The Moirai sisters?"

Roman doesn't have to confirm that I'm right because nothing he can say will ease any amount of dread I'm feeling right now. His creators... his family so to speak, are the vilest of gods. I swallow hard, remembering the essay I wrote in high school about Erebus, the mother of the Fates, and how she was primeval of void and chaos, the epitome of hell, along with her siblings and children. My teacher told me I was wrong, but standing here with Roman proves differently.

"Pure evil."

"I'm not," Roman reaches for my hand. I'm tempted to pull away, but I need the comfort he can provide. He's right though, he's not evil. In the short amount of time I've met him, he hasn't done anything wrong, except almost killing my father. I want to pull him into my arms, but the thought of him being with Selene still lingers in my mind.

"Tell me about Selene." Roman puts some distance

between us. It's all I need to know. They've been together. I shouldn't care, but I do. "Were you bonded?"

He shakes his head. "No, vampires can't bond to one another."

"So you can't marry your kind?"

"We can and do, but it's not something I want. Bonding is the strongest emotion we have, and we all yearn to feel a connection with a mortal."

I hate that we keep getting off topic. "You've been with her though?"

"Like I said when the Sisters let us go, it's a frenzy with heightened senses beyond anything a mortal could ever experience. As it was, Selene and I woke up in the seediest part of a town in England. Everything around us was sex and murder. These men talking about the newest prostitute at the brothel or how they shot someone in battle and held their foot over their heart until they stopped breathing. These men catered to our new instincts, but we didn't know what to do or how to hone them.

"When a vampire is created, they're assigned a mentor of sorts. When our mentor found us, he made us follow him to meet with this consort. Like children, we were made to sit outside the room while he fucked her, but the sounds and smells... the urges became too much, too painful to resist. Unsure of what to do, Selene and I acted. As I said we're left with very instincts, some stronger than others."

Roman's word sink in. He's been with Selene. It could be once, or twice or some on going affair. I have so many questions. How long? When was the last time? Is she some side piece I have to worry about when we're not together? He comes to me, placing his hands on my arms.

"Your anger is rolling off you in droves, my love. The

last few days, I've thrown a lot at you about my life. Please talk to me."

"I hate that you've been with her," I seethe.

"And I hate that the human known as Shan knows you intimately as well. Each time I see him, I want to rip him apart. I know there are more men out there who have touched you, been buried deep inside of you, and made you scream their names, and each day I fight the urge to hunt them down because I don't want to hurt you. Selene is a friend, nothing more and will never be. We do not look at each other this way."

"But there are others."

Roman smiles. "Women? Of course, there are. I've walked this earth for five hundred years and have never claimed to be celibate."

"How can I be sure they won't come looking for you?"

"The same way I can't be sure one of your lovers won't come and try to steal you away from me, and before you tell me that'll never happen, I know it can. I've seen it. Humans can request that a bond is broken." Roman cups my cheek and pulls me to him. Our bodies crash into each other, and while I expect him to pick me up and take me to his bedroom, he doesn't. Instead, he leans in and whispers, "The reason I keep checking my phone is that I'm waiting for word that the Sisters are gone."

"Are they?"

He shrugs, which is one of the cutest humanely things he does. It's the simple things in Roman that I find attractive. "I don't know, but the clouds are lifting, and I think it's time to venture out into the world."

"Really? You don't want to stay in?"

"Can you do me a favor?"

"Anything," I tell him.

"Come with me to Clutch and talk to Selene. I think that if you know her a little better, and she you, you'd feel more comfortable around each other."

"Roman..."

"Please, Fiona. I wouldn't ask if it weren't important."

I take a step back and gather my thoughts. I want to tell him no and ask that he stay away from Clutch, but Lydia's words are pressing into the forefront of my thoughts. At Clutch, the vampires can be themselves. They don't have to hide or pretend. But Selene... that is where I'm torn. I shouldn't care, but I do. Truthfully, I'm jealous.

"Fiona?" Roman pleads. I nod, but even as I do, I'm second-guessing everything. In a flash, Roman has me in his arms. "Hang on, we're going to run." I do as he says, barely able to make out the sound of his door and the door to the building stairs opening and closing, along with the noise from the Strip. For the most part, Roman tries to be human, taking a cab to and from places or even driving if the occasion calls for it. With no concept of how long or rather how quickly it's taken us, we're at the door of Clutch and Roman is removing my necklace.

"Corban, right?" The vampire sneers but doesn't say anything. I know it has to do with my cross, but I don't care. When I'm not with Roman, it gives me a sense of security. Roman's usual chatty self doesn't say anything to Corban before we enter the club.

The last time I was here, it was busy, with humans sitting at the bar and a line of foot traffic heading to the back area. Tonight, it'd dead, no pun intended, except Selene being behind the bar and a DJ in the corner playing music.

Selene glares at me or through me. I can't be sure, but the thought of talking to her right now doesn't sit well with me. "Let's dance," Roman says, tearing me away from

Selene. It's probably for the best. She'd destroy me without blinking an eye. I'm sure she's laughing, on the inside, because she shows zero emotion whatsoever. In all likelihood, she probably doesn't care that I have a slight issue with her sleeping with Roman. I don't care if it happened eons ago, it still happened, and they're still close.

Roman all but picks me up and carries me to the dance floor where he spins me into his arms.

"Something tells me you know every type of dance out there."

"Except break dancing. I may be immortal, but the thought of getting on the ground to spin never appealed to me."

"In middle and high school, we're forced to learn swing dancing. As if we're not already awkward, but to be forced to hold hands with a boy..." I shiver at the thought, remembering the cooties infested boy I had to dance with back in sixth grade.

Roman and I sway to the music. My fingers play with the fine hairs on the back of his neck and trailing to his stubble. I'm thankful that the Sister changed him while he had the makings of a beard growing.

When the song changes, he pulls me closer, pressing himself into me. "Can I tell you something?"

"You can tell me anything," he says.

"I think I'm falling in love with you."

27

ROMAN

*I*f I had chosen a more subservient human to bond with, I'd be able to keep her with me at all times where I can protect her and watch over her, but that's not what I did. I chose a human with a stubbornness that is unrivaled. Fiona insists that she needs to go home and do human things that I wouldn't understand, although I think she forgets that I was human at one point. Albeit a long time ago, I was human nonetheless.

It has been good for Fiona and me to spend the few days that we did together, alone. She started to call it "cooped up," but I can see she doesn't completely understand the seriousness of the Sisters visit. In over five hundred years, I'd never met them, and I hope that in the next five hundred I don't need to again. Once the clouds lifted and the power came back on entirely, my apprehension faded and while not my preference, I let Fiona leave to handle her business.

I'm going to ask her to move in with me soon. I've been thinking about it for awhile now, and I love her completely. She belongs to me, where I can protect her and look after her. If I had a human heart, it would have jumped from my chest when she told me she was falling in love with me. She works so hard to protect her feelings, to not be vulnerable, I feared she might never truly love me the way I love her. If I could find a way to spend my eternity with her, I would do it in a second. But I will make her my everything for the time we do have together. Her family situation's still unresolved, and I neglected to talk to her more in-depth about the conversation she had with her father. When she is with me, I tend to get lost in her.

Since Fiona left, and I have my own business to attend to, I call Melody's office to arrange a meeting. It's been far too long since I've received an update, and I want to know what's going on with my license, and the sale of the casino. We haven't made any progress on the applications, and I'm determined not to have a human partner still, so I'd like to hear in person whether or not we are at a standstill. I'm sure I'm going to get some song and dance about the power outage and such, but this deal is taking far too long, and I do not have a good feeling about it. As much as I know it will upset Fiona, I am prepared to do what needs to be done to finalize this sale, and if that means a meeting with her father myself, I intend to do it. I'm not about to let a fat, aging crook dictate how this is going to go down.

I can't compel him; he wears a cross, and I'm not about getting beheaded in front of my peers by any of the Sisters, but I don't think I'd get in trouble if I made a threat. I wouldn't kill him over this, but I'm not above playing the role of the monster that I can be when provoked, mainly to get what I need. That singular human is not going to be the reason I don't get what I want, and Fiona will learn to forgive me if things escalate.

Melody gets back to me and indicates that she is at her

office but can meet me out for a drink, which I have no use for if I'd like. I have no use for a drink, so I let her know I'll be coming to her office. Her inability to remember basic common facts about vampires is annoying, especially since she apparently wants to fuck me. You'd think she'd remember some details. If I had nerves to get on, all humans except Fiona would be on them right now. My perception of their inferiority has risen to the surface since the power outage. They scatter like ants, and I have a growing desire to crush them.

Since I have all day to myself, I take the human route to Melody's office across town. Traffic is a nightmare as it tends to be most of the time in Las Vegas, although sitting in the back of a taxi gives me the opportunity to observe what's happening on the Strip. After a few days of chaos, an uptick in looting and crime from the outages, it seems that things are back to normal. Families are walking about taking pictures, whores are on the street corners handing out cards, and gamblers are parading in and out of the casinos like normal. The only indication that anything had happened in the last few days is the three bodegas I see that have a broken window boarded up, but it's hardly noticeable unless you are looking for it. The greed and the gluttony are back at the forefront, just another day in Sin City.

I walk into Melody's office, which is a storefront in a strip mall. Typically, I would deal with a business that had a more significant office, a more sophisticated longstanding look to it, but her firm has helped other vampires with great success, and that is good enough for me. The receptionist greets me with lust in her eyes.

"Good afternoon, Roman."

"Good afternoon. I'm here to see Melody." I have no interest in waiting, and surely she knows this. She doesn't speak, as if she's in a trance, staring at me. Weak humans do this. You don't even have to compel them, they practically compel themselves. Her red hair reminds me of Lachesis and is falling in tendrils around her face which I find disturbing. My eyes scan her neck, where I can see the variety of different bite marks, indicative of being bitten by many vampires, in various stages of healing. Patience thinning, I tap my finger on the counter to snap her back to my needs. "Where is she?"

"Oh, I'm sorry. I'll call Mel."

"No need." I walk past the little counter. I'm not going to sit in the waiting area like a commoner while she buzzes Melody, whose heartbeat I can hear from where I stand.

Melody looks up from her desk as if she is surprised to see me, and she immediately begins fidgeting.

"Roman, hi there! Have a seat." She gestures to the chair across from her desk. I sense something isn't right, and my patience is growing thin already.

"What is going on with my property?"

"Well, it's been a crazy couple of days with the power outages and electrical storm--"

I interrupt her. "That has no significance in my business, Melody. What is going on with my property? You are not telling me something." I lean in, narrowing my eyes at her, compelling her. I'm done being tolerant and accommodating today; something isn't right, and I want to know what it is now.

Entirely under my control now, her voice is even and serene. "There has been another bid. Someone outbid you on the property."

I slam my fist down violently on her desk, cracking the fake wood. "Who is it!?" I demand.

The fear evident as her lip trembles, she replies. "I don't

know. The bidder was anonymous. I have no way of finding out who it is. These things are sealed. But we can enter a new bid and go from there if you wish, but this doesn't solve our issue of... the license." She's scared, and it fuels me to an extent. It feels good to be angry, the hate flowing through me like fire.

"I don't care about this fucking license! Find out who is trying to steal my property from me. I will take care of the license myself. I'm done playing games and waiting around, Melody; do you understand me?"

"Yes Roman, but I don't know... I don't have a way to get the information you're looking for. I'm just a broker..." Her fear is real, and I use it to my advantage.

"You will figure it out. And you will get it fucking handled. Do you understand me? This is not a request any longer. It is a demand, and you will obey me." The venom flowing from me is potent, and watching her tremble pleases me. I'm furious she allowed this to happen, and if it were three hundred years ago, I'd rip her throat out, feed on her and leave her drained corpse as a lesson to the others.

"I understand," she whispers.

"I will be back. Get this taken care of." I need to feed, now. My anger is overwhelming, and my thirst needs to be satiated immediately. I storm from the office, slamming the glass door behind me, which shatters.

I head to Clutch on foot, not even attempting to calm my anger. She had one fucking job, and in typical lazy human fashion, she has failed me. It's a long walk to the bar, but it gives me time to think of a new plan. It's time for Mr. Weston to have a one on one with yours truly. I'll put another bid in, that's fine I have the money, but I'm done fucking around with human bureaucracy. I don't want to lose Fiona, so I need to calculate how this will go down, and I'll do that after I feed.

Storming past Corban, I go directly to Selene with impatience.

"I need to feed. Now."

Crossing her arms petulantly at me, she grins. "Oh, Fiona out of fuel?"

"Not now, Selene. Get me someone."

Realizing that I'm not interested in our usual banter, she comes out from behind the bar and stands next to me. "You know how this works, go pick one. They're all ready and willing participants, Roman," she whispers, gesturing around the room at the primarily female humans all anxiously awaiting a bite.

"Not a woman. It needs to be a human man."

"Interesting choice, Roman. You switching teams now?" She smirks at me playfully.

"Enough!" I hiss at her. "I made a promise to Fiona I would not feed on another woman. Find me a man. Now!" I demand again.

Rolling her eyes at my attitude, she huffs. "Fine. Go in the back. Room four. I'll send someone back to you in a minute. Lose the attitude while you're back there."

I don't respond and storm to the back where feeding rooms are lined up in what's almost a mini hotel hallway. Each room has a bed, a couch, and a first aid kit in case things get out of hand. I want to bite, my anger bringing out my animal needs.

A knock at the door grabs my attention. "Enter," I say.

The door opens toward me, and standing before me is a young man, no more than twenty-five. Well dressed and handsome, he has innocence in his eyes as if he's not done this before. Setting my concerns aside, my eyes scan to his neck and see his jugular pulsing.

"I'm Nicolai. I'm here to feed you," he says, no reservation in his voice. Still standing in the doorway, he must be waiting for me to say something.

"Come here," I growl, exposing my fangs. "Shut the door behind you and lock it."

28

FIONA

I haven't seen Leslie since she found out about Roman and me, but I called her anyway to join Lana and me for a bit of retail therapy. Of course, I've gotten in the habit of keeping my fang marks hidden, at least from the public. Roman doesn't know about the cream I bought, and I'm trying to keep it that way because I don't want him to think I'm ashamed. I'm not. I'm scared of what my father might do if he finds out I'm still seeing Roman.

Lana squeals when she sees me. We hug in the middle of the store, much to the annoyance of the clerk, who is huffing as she walks by. Mentally, I flip her off. Between Lana and I, we're about to spend a boatload of money in here, which will probably give the clerk a nice commission check.

"I'm so happy you called, I have news."

"You're pregnant," I say, jokingly. Unless Lana has ditched her vampire trainer boyfriend, there's no way she could be pregnant, right? The thought makes me go still. Roman and I don't use protection, and I'm assuming he's sterile because technically he's dead and... my hand presses against my abdomen as I silently tick off the days since my last period. "Oh, God."

Lana shakes her head. "I'm not, are you?"

I look at her and see nothing but horror stretched across her face. I cover my mouth, and we quickly exit the store and rush through the casino to the elevators. Lana presses the button repeatedly as if doing so will make the lift move faster. My stomach's queasy and my legs are quivering. I hate this feeling except for when Roman is the one making them shake uncontrollably due to the orgasm he's given me. What if...? No, I can't think like that.

Lana and I step into the elevator. She holds my hand, trying to reassure me, but it's not working. "You haven't used condoms, huh?" she asks as soon as the last person steps off.

I shake my head. "I didn't think we had to."

Lana sighs. "I've heard of women carrying half vampire babies. Some die in childbirth."

"Who, the mom or the baby?"

"The mom," she says quietly.

We arrive at my floor and quickly rush to my apartment and into the bathroom where I drop to my knees and rifle through the cabinet under my sink. "I know I have a test in here."

"Do you think it's the same? I mean, can it tell if you're pregnant with a vampire baby?"

"I don't know, but I'm going to try. I have to know." Lana leaves me to pee on the stick. After I do, I set it on the counter and wash my hands, refusing to look at it, knowing deep down I'm screwed.

Roman and I just met. Our relationship is far too early to bring a child into it, and what would I tell my father? He will surely disown me for getting knocked up by a vampire.

I open the door and let Lana in. She immediately goes to the stick and watches it. I don't want to know if it's changing because I already know I'm pregnant. I should've had my period by now.

"Not pregnant," Lana says.

"What?"

"It says not pregnant."

I breathe a massive sigh of relief, and instantly tears start to stream down my face. "Hey," Lana whispers. "It's okay. Now you know how you feel if you were to get pregnant, but you can't."

"What do you mean?"

"I texted my guy and asked. He said it's not allowed unless permission is sought from one of the Sisters, and if they agree, it's a ritual. So you're safe. We're all safe."

"Yeah, I suppose you're right." Reality sure has a funny way of showing you how screwed up your decisions are. I'm bonded to a man who can't give me children unless he seeks permission from the crazy freaks who created him. And up until I took the test, I wasn't sure I wanted children, but now maybe I do, but I'd never ask Roman to ask the Sisters for help. Hell no, not after what he's told me.

I take a deep calming breath and deduce that if Roman and I are to continue, we'll adopt a child. There's plenty of children in the orphanage who need good, loving homes, which Roman and I can provide for them. And if the time comes when I need to experience childbirth, we'll talk about a sperm donor, but until then, I'm going to focus on being in love with my sexy vampire and help him build an empire.

At Lana's encouragement, we return to the mall. Leslie's there, waiting for us, and truthfully, I forgot all about her in my panic. "Where were you? I tried calling."

"I'm sorry," I say, kissing her on the cheek. "I had to run up to my apartment quickly."

"For what?" she asks.

Lie, Fiona. Lie like you've never lied before. "I forgot my phone." My voice rises when I say phone, a sure sign that I'm full of shit and Leslie knows it.

"I see." She smiles, but it doesn't reach her cheeks. Fuck my life.

"Let's shop, shall we?" Lana says, trying to save the day. Together the three of us browse the racks with the latest fashions. Every so often, I look over my shoulder to see if Roman's out there, watching me. I don't sense him, but ever since the Sisters' visit, I've felt sort of off when it comes to him.

Store after store, we buy up the newest trends, loading our arms with bags of items we don't need. "I'm going to have to spend the weekend cleaning out my closet."

"My mom is hosting a charity auction in a month; you could donate your old stuff to her," Lana says.

"That sounds about perfect." I look down at the many bags, wishing Roman would appear and help me carry these to my apartment. As if on cue, the energy I feel when he's near piques. If it were only Lana, I'd seek him out, but with Leslie here, I can't. "I think I'm going to go. My arms are getting tired, and I have to start planning the next investor party."

"Has your dad decided to issue a license yet for the Majesty?"

I shake my head, even though he told me I could have it. I have yet to hear back on the bid I put in and whether it's been accepted. "I'm sure whoever pads his pockets the most will walk away with the prized paper."

"Do you want some help?" Leslie asks. Her hands are as

full as mine, so I'm not sure how'd she help me. I glance over my shoulder, sensing Roman is near and spot him looking into the window of the store, pretending to ignore us. Thankfully, Leslie has no idea what Roman looks like so she hasn't caught on to the fact he's standing behind us.

"I'm fine, you go on ahead. I can always ask the bellhop to take my bags up."

The three of us say goodbye and promise to catch up. I stand in the middle of the mall, watching my friends leave, both avoiding each other.

"Let me take those." His silky voice sends shivers down my spine. I'm tempted to tell him about today, but it's a conversation for later in life, after we've been together for a while. Although, I'm going to have to hide the evidence when we get upstairs, not that Roman has any reason to use my bathroom.

I turn and fall into his arms. His scent surrounds me, making me feel at peace. "I've missed you."

"I missed you, too."

When I pull away, I see the remnants of dried blood in the corner of his mouth. My jaw clenches as I step away and look over his shoulder. Words escape me right now. I don't know what to say. First, he disappears, going radio silent for days and now he's fed off someone. "I have to go."

I rush toward the casino, weaving in and out of gamblers and tourists. Roman is calling after me, but I don't stop. I can't, although I know, he can catch me anytime he wants, putting me at a disadvantage in our relationship. I'm still two steps ahead when the elevator door is about to close, barely stepping on in time. Roman's face is the last thing I see as the doors close.

Luck isn't on my side, at least not today. I should've known he'd take the stairs to beat me to my apartment.

Sometimes, he doesn't play fair. I guess that's the nature of the game when dating a vampire. "I can't talk to you right now."

"Then you'll listen," he says, following me inside. He slams the door, and I jump.

"I want you to leave." By law, he has to do what I say, although it's a dumb law since no one can enforce it. If the police were to show up, he could compel them to believe he means no harm, and I'd be left with trying to plead with a human zombie.

Roman moves lightning fast to stand in front of me. His hands are holding my arms to my side. The blood I saw earlier, is now gone, making me more disgusted. "Did you fuck her?" I spit out.

"No, and if you'd give me a minute to explain."

"I saw the evidence, Roman. What are you going to say, your teeth slipped?"

He actually laughs, even though I don't find it funny. "You're a spitfire, you know that."

"At least I'm not a cheater."

Roman nods. "The fact that you think I would cheat on you, to break the bond we share, is laughable and yet, heart-breaking. I didn't cheat. I didn't bite another female. I went to Clutch to feed after I found out some very upsetting news in regards to my business dealings. I chose a man to sate my thirst. Not a woman. I would never do that to you, Fiona." His grip on my arms loosens as he relaxes a bit.

"Are you...?" I swallow hard. "Do you like men?"

He shakes his head. "No. I'm all for your tantalizing pussy and your glorious jugular. I need no one else to satisfy me."

"Okay." I pull Roman into a hug and tell him I'm sorry, showering him with kisses."I'm sorry for accusing you,

Roman. Let me make it up to you. Let me feed you." My jumping to conclusions needs to stop. I need to trust Roman. Trust him when he tells me he won't do anything to hurt me. When I go to pull his shirt off, he stops me.

"I'm sorry, I need to calm down before I fuck you."

"Why?" I ask.

"Because today hasn't been very good, Fiona. Coupled with the fact you thought I cheated on you, I'm a bit agitated right now, and I'm afraid I might hurt you."

"Oh. Is there anything I can do?"

He shakes his head. "Tell me everything's going to work out."

"I mean, sure? Maybe you should tell me what's going on." I move over to the couch and sit down, waiting for Roman to follow. After a long beat, he finally does but leaves too much space between us.

"I went and saw my real estate agent today and found out I was outbid. So while I'm being patient and waiting, someone swooped in and put more money on the table. I don't know how much it's going to cost me, but I'm at my breaking point, Fiona. If you can't get your father to give me the license I need, I'm going to pay him a visit."

Roman's angry, this much I can gather by the tone of his voice. Usually, he speaks to me softly, but not now. Each word is harsh, threatening. I don't know how I'm going to tell him I'm the one who outbid him on his project to ensure he received the license. "Um... Roman, I have something to say."

"What is it?"

I clear my throat and instead of sitting up to face my vampire, I slink back into the cushion. I had no idea this would upset him so much. I tell him about the visit with my father and how I presented the project as my own so I could assure that my father would issue the license, and how my dad is completely on board. "This way, you get what you want."

In the time it takes to blink, my coffee table, chair, and wet bar are shattered into pieces. I cower and use my arms to shield my head. "YOU," he roars. "You've defied and stolen from me."

"It's not like that, Roman. I'm trying to help because I believe in what you want to do and I know my father will never issue anything to a vampire, let alone the one who to tried to kill him and is screwing his daughter."

Roman picks me up, his eyes are beady slits, and for the first time, I'm terrified for my life. "I'm done with this." He tosses me onto the couch like a rag doll, and storms out of my apartment, slamming the door so hard it splinters. I call out to him, but it's no use. He's gone. "Oh, God, what have I done?"

29

ROMAN

I can't believe she's defied me this way. I'm starting to think Selene's right when she said human consorts are nothing but trouble, like having babies that need to be taken care of. They have an inability to see our differences because of our human appearance except when it suits them. I storm from her house to mine where I pace feverishly, wringing my hands. I'm trying to calm down, to formulate a plan of action, but all I feel is nothing but betrayal.

I can just outbid her, there's no way she has enough money to beat me in a bidding war, but she's taken my plans as her own without consulting me. Not only is this a violation of her role in a multitude of ways, but it's also just shitty. She says she loves me, but how is stealing my plans love? It's not. Even a vampire knows this.

I can't think straight, and I decide that being alone is simply making me crazy, and being with humans is off the table right now. I'm so pissed that I head back to Clutch. While Selene will likely just tell me she knew this would happen, she's my kind, and she will know what to do.

When I arrive, Corban is standing outside as usual. "Back again so soon?" he asks.

"Yeah, my afternoon plans fell through," I lie. He doesn't need to know my tale right now, and I'm pretending I'm not in the mood to rip this whole fucking city apart right now.

"What are you doing back here?" Selene raises an eyebrow from her seat at the far end of the bar where she was talking to an attractive bartender I've never seen before.

"Long story." I want to tell her what's going on, but I'm so angry I need to just sit for a moment.

"Go." She gestures for the young lady to leave. "Something's happened. What is it?" I'm not sure if her concern is for me, or something else.

"I was outbid on my casino project," I reply.

"Seriously, Roman? That's your problem? You have plenty of money. This is a problem you can throw human money at to fix. You're really turning into an emotional human." Her sarcasm isn't lost on me, and I narrow my eyes at her.

"I was outbid by Fiona."

Selene's dark eyes widen, and a smirk forms. "Well, well, well. It seems the little angel has a dark side after all. Why on earth did she do that?"

"She did it so that the license would be granted to her since she is a human."

"Well, I hate to take her side, because... well, because I don't care for the whole human-vampire relationship. However, she's right. She did this for you. What are you so pissed off about? Is this male ego bullshit? If it is, go find someone else to talk to, or I'll have to fight you out back like it's the seventeenth century and remind you who's stronger."

Well aware that Selene is stronger than I am, I'd rather not have my ass kicked today on top of everything else that's happened. "It's not my ego, it's her defiance. She should have discussed this with me. She continues to jump to conclusions and make assumptions, and I'm done with it."

"I'm quite sure you're not done with it, but why don't you go get one of the consorts and relieve some stress? Get a little drink." She winks at me as if we are talking about a refreshing cocktail of some kind.

"I've already fed today, I don't need more."

"You're allowed a treat now and again, Roman. Feeding more than you need to sometimes feels so good." She licks her red lips, her fangs peeking out just a bit. "You're always so stuffy. What you need is to fuck it out, but I'm sure you're still committed to your little mortal, so go get some juice. It'll take the edge off."

I contemplate what she says. Rarely do I feed more than I need to for survival. It provides a bit of a euphoric, almost drunken state for a brief period of time, and it can be incredibly addicting if you don't keep it in check. I'm angry with Fiona, and while I said that I was done, I shouted it in anger, not in truth. I won't fuck someone else, but I will feed again. Nicolai was clean, young and delicious. And he was soft spoken and agreeable even when I was rough with him earlier.

"Where's Nicolai? I want him," I demand, a thirst rising inside me.

Selene, my good friend, and the worst influence narrows her eyes and grins. "Now we're talking. There's the vampire I know and love. I will send him back to you."

I walk back to the same room that I was with him in earlier and look around. It's been cleaned, even though we didn't leave a mess behind. I haven't done it in a long time, but there was a time that I might visit a room like this with a woman, and bite, and fuck and bite and fuck for hours, which could very well leave a bit of a mess.

Nicolai's soft knock on the door brings my thoughts back to the now. Part of me knows I need to be careful, a feeding frenzy can get out of hand quickly. But the other part of me needs the high. Like Selene said, to take the edge off. He enters the room, looking at me quizzically.

"I understand you requested to see me?" he asks.

"I did, Nicolai. I want more. Do you have more to give me?" I ask, examining his features. He's young but has the mannerisms of someone who's been taught how to behave appropriately, almost subserviently. If I were into men, he would appeal to me. I like pussy far too much to switch though.

"It would be my pleasure to service you, Roman," he says, smiling.

Service me. Yes, that's what I need. To be serviced; to be in charge. I move to the couch and sit, motioning for the young man to kneel before me. It feels good to get my way. "I want to taste you again, now," I demand gruffly.

Nicolai faces me and rests his hands on my thighs. I observe him, he's not new to this, and yet retains an innocence as he moves closer to me. I lean forward, tilting his neck to the side, examining the marks I left earlier. I lick them again, to help them heal, causing him to suck in a breath. It occurs to me that he enjoys this, and I may as well enjoy it too, after all, it's not cheating. I grab a fistful of his hair, roughly holding him in place, and sink my teeth into a new spot. As his blood begins to flow, coating my tongue and filling my mouth, I groan.

The euphoric feeling sets in quickly. It's only been a few hours since I'd had any, and it was far more than I needed. As a human, I don't believe I used any illicit drugs, and they didn't exist as they do now, but I would imagine this overwhelming sensation is what keeps addicts coming back for more. I continue to drink, binging on him until he grabs my legs so tightly, I stop to see what's wrong.

I made a terrible miscalculation. The life force is leaving Nicolai's eyes. I rise up in a panic. "Fuck," I mutter as he slumps onto the floor in a heap.

Quickly, I run to get Selene. I drank too much, and he's close to being drained; she will know what to do. When she arrives in the doorway, she takes one look at Nicolai and pulls me back into the room, slamming the door behind us.

"What have you done, Roman?"

"I don't know. It was a mistake! We have to do something!" I exclaim. I knew this was a bad idea. Fuck my life. Fiona won't have to forgive me for killing a human because the Sisters are going to kill me anyway.

Selene drops to her knees and starts performing CPR on him. "He's not responding, Roman. This is so fucked up. So. Fucked. Up." She is angry, and I'm freaking out when suddenly she freezes. Her actions halt, and she stands up, ramming herself against the wall of the room as if someone shoved her there. Her gaze is blank, staring off into space.

The next thing I know, the door flies open, and the Sisters are in the room. All three of them, standing before me, with blood dripping down my chin and a dead or dying human at my feet. I am so fucked.

Atropos grabs me by the neck, shoving me into the wall next to Selene, her nails burning into my skin. "What have you done, Roman?!" she demands.

"I... It was an accident. He is still alive!" I choke out, her strength far more significant than mine.

All three Sisters look at Nicolai, who's flat on his back

and clinging to life. Atropos still holds me to the wall, where Selene is seemingly suspended in place as if to be kept out of the way. Lachesis lets out a cackle of a laugh, startling me; the noise apparently causes her sisters to smile. Their evil grins all turn back to me.

"We will make him reborn," she says, her wicked laugh following her statement.

"Yes!" Atropos agrees.

"Oh! A new child! How very exciting!" Clothos clasps her hands together enthusiastically. "I want him to keep his human name. I adore the name Nicolai." Her childlike nature is disturbing.

"Humans receive new names, that is our rule," Lachesis replies.

"But I like his name. It's perfect for him. Look at that sweet face of his." Clothos leans down to touch his face, stroking it gently. I'm choking less now, but I dare not move, for I don't know what my fate is.

"Keep his name. I don't care. We make the rules. Now, what do we do with this one? Death seems like such an easy way out for him." Atropos turns her attention back to me.

"I agree," Lachesis says.

"He will become Nicolai's watcher." Atropos lets me down, and Selene falls to the floor, waking from her trance and looking utterly confused at the same time.

"Oh yes, this is wonderful!" Clotho kneels beside Nicolai and begins to wave her hands over him as if she's putting a spell on him. "He is just barely still human, we must do this quickly."

Atropos moves beside Nicolai, grabbing his wrist violently, as it begins to let off smoke. The smell of burning flesh fills the room. His skin pales further, and any life that appeared to be left in him fades with her grip. "He is ready." She looks to Lachesis, who is standing by, watching.

The mark of the Fates is left where Atropos held Nicolai's wrist, embedded into his skin for eternity. I've never seen a vampire made, and it's not lost on me that I was once in Nicolai's place. I turn my attention to Selene, who is watching in horror as Lachesis takes Atropos's spot, kneeling next to Nicolai. Lachesis extends her arm out over him, and with the other, slices her own wrist, causing a steady stream of blood to flow. As it drips off her arm, she positions it over Nicolai, letting it stream directly into his mouth.

Within moments, his eyes fly open, and he sits upright, his gray eyes as huge as can be. Selene and I both step back, as Clothos begins to clap in delight.

"Oh, my baby! So precious, my Nicolai!" she exclaims. She's crazier than I imagined even possible, her childlike behavior bordering on psychotic now. The Sisters all stand across from Selene and me, while Nicolai pushes himself up off the floor, holding his throat with one hand. "He's thirsty! We must get him something to drink. Keeper!" she yells at Selene. "Go fetch a human for him to feed. Now!"

Selene runs from the room, and the Sisters all turn to me. "You are responsible for his well being. For teaching him our ways. If anything happens to him, you will die a thousand deaths, do you understand?" Atropos says to me.

Fuck. Me. Did I just become a dad to a fucking vampire coed? "Yes, I understand," is my reply.

"That is not your only punishment. Your human will suffer for your actions as well. The bond you share will be broken, and she will receive a visit... from us." Atropos and Lachesis cackle together, while Clotho is obsessively watching Nicolai, who is now cowering on the bed in the tiny room, likely wondering what the fuck is going on.

"Please leave Fi—"

"Enough! You do not get a say in what happens here. You've done enough. Now tend to your apprentice!" Atropos yells at me. I stand subservient and nod, but I am not going to let them do anything to Fiona.

"Goodbye, my child. Enjoy yourself here on Earth. The spoils of our wars are yours in which to take delight in," Clothos addresses Nicolai as she prepares to leave.

"We will be watching, Roman. Do not defy us," Atropos threatens, as the door opens on its own, and the Sisters float out of the room.

Fucking fuck. This is so fucking bad. I look over at Nicolai, who appears both confused and scared, and I know that he needs to feed immediately. Selene comes back, clutching the arm of a young female consort, and together we teach Nicolai how to feed.

30

FIONA

"*T*hanks, guys," I say to the team who rushed up here to install a new door. All while they were here I had to fight back my tears. I couldn't let them know my vampire lover did this, they'd have him banned from the property, and I can't have that. Although, I have a feeling Roman isn't coming back.

I thought I was doing the right thing by presenting Roman's project to my father. I believe in Roman so much, I only wanted to help, and I know my dad will not work with a vampire. If Roman were to compel my father... well, I suspect my dad would turn Roman in, and I can't have that. It seems now though, it doesn't matter what I want. My good deed wasn't what Roman wanted, which makes me wonder, did he really want me or was I the ticket to get his gaming license?

I step out onto my balcony and notice the dark clouds rolling over the Strip. Down on the street, people scatter, looking for cover from the impending rain, but these clouds don't bring rain, they bring fear. I remember them distinctly from before, when Roman disappeared, and now they're back. I've never believed in omens until now. Something terrible is about to happen, and I'm going to be all alone, stuck in my penthouse, not knowing what's going on and with no vampire to turn to.

Stepping back inside, I lock the sliding glass door and press the button to darken the windows, but nothing happens. Already, the power surge is starting. It's only a matter of time before city and state officials begin to ask questions as to what's going on and why. Who's going to answer them? Will a vampire step forward and tell the government that their creators got a wild hair up their ass and came to Las Vegas to party? What, if anything, can the humans even do?

"Nothing," I say aloud. "There isn't a damn thing anyone can do." Roman can preach equality all he wants, but his creators, the Sisters, as he calls them, rule the world. They aren't following any human laws because surely depleting our energy and making us prisoners in our own homes while they conduct business would be highly frowned upon. Call me crazy, but I don't think this is part of the ancient pact they signed.

I resign myself to the fact that I'm stuck here until the witches of the underworld finish their business and go back to wherever it is they live. It's been a while since I read, and pick the book up off my nightstand and situate myself on the couch. Only, once I open the book, I realize I don't have a lamp on my end table because some temperamental vampire threw a temper tantrum and destroyed my furniture.

Crying out in frustration, I throw my book across the room and head back out to my balcony where the dark clouds have cooled off the sweltering heat. It's only a matter of time before what's left of the coldness from the air conditioner will turn warm, leaving us no choice but to seek refuge outside.

Instead of sitting, I watch the people down below. I count three traffic accidents already, with more to come. Above me, on the roof, someone is yelling about aliens coming, and the only thing I can think is that their arrival would be welcomed right now. Maybe they could give the evil triplets a run for their money.

There's a loud screech; the noise reverberates through my head. I close my eyes and press my temples to push it away, but it only becomes louder, harder. Almost as if something is in my brain, trying to escape. I scream out and fall to my knees, my hands cradling my head while my fingers dig into my skin. Then suddenly, it stops, and I'm floating. My feet dangle below me as I hover over the Strip, suspended in the air by nothing. I run in place, trying to get back to my terrace, but nothing happens. I reach for the railing, hoping to grab, to give me something to hold onto, but I can't. I'm frozen, mid-air, hundreds of feet above the ground.

"What the fuck is happening?" I yell up to the sky, hoping some god will take pity on me and set me down safely onto solid ground.

There's childish laughter coming from my apartment, but I can't see who is making the noise. Not that I can do much from where I am, but I call out, "Who's there?" Big mistake as three of the most beautiful women I have ever seen appears in my doorway. There isn't a single doubt in my mind who these women are. My only question is, why are they here? Actually, I take that back. I have another question, why are they doing this to me?

"Hello Sisters," I say, to be pleasant. The last thing I want is to piss them off. They already have me by the proverbial balls.

"You know us?" the one with jet black hair down to her waist says as she angles her head slightly.

"It seems the consort knows more than she should," the redhead surmises.

Fuck my life and my nosey ways.

"Can we play with her?" the last one asks, clapping her hands.

"NO!" the darker-haired one screams, making it sound like thunder. My entire life, I've been told thunder is the angels bowling and lightning is a strike. Guess I was wrong. Before I know, I'm in front of the Sisters, being inspected. They circle me, poking and prodding. One traces Roman's faded teeth marks on my neck.

"She feeds your son well, Clotho. You should be proud."

Is there a wrong way to feed a vampire? Surely, he dictates everything.

"We should take her with us. Make her our servant."

Um, no. This human is perfectly happy to stay right here.

"We have no use for a human. Stop playing with her so we can break the bond and move on. I'm bored." The sister with the black hair, I deduce is in charge, but I don't like what she says about breaking the bond I have with Roman.

Swiftly, I'm brought into my house and sat in a chair, yet I still cannot move. It feels like there are a million tons of weight holding me down, yet I don't feel any pressure, just paralyzed. "Can someone please tell me what's going on?"

"My Roman has been a naughty boy tonight, and now you must die," the blonde says. The way she says die, it sounds like she's happy she's about to murder me.

"I have to die because Roman's bad?" I ask, hedging my bets. "Doesn't Roman have free will?" The redhead points her finger at me, I watch as it turns into a blade. "Holy mother of..." If I didn't see it with my own eyes, I would have never believed any of this was true. "I don't understand, what did I do to deserve death?"

"Humans live to serve the needs of a vampire. When a vampire chooses to take a consort, said consort must follow our Covenant. Roman broke the gravest of rules this evening and must pay the price. The only consequence he cares for is you, and therefore, we must end your existence. Roman will walk the earth in solitary pain until he meets his doom."

My eyes go wide as the black-haired sister tells me why I must die. Roman's decision to be a dick has backfired in more ways than one. If he would've just listened to me earlier and accepted what I had done for him, instead of pitching a fit, I wouldn't be here right now.

The Sisters approach and start to circle around me. One has her hands waving around while the others chant in a language I've never heard. The energy I usually feel from Roman increases, making me feel like it's about to burst out of me. "What are you doing?" I grit out.

No one answers.

They stop suddenly, and I burst into tears. There's something wrong. I can feel it. "I don't want to die," I mutter. "Please."

"Stop!"

My head jerks up at the sound of Roman's voice. He's not alone though, there's another man with him. Did he bring back-up?

"Nicolai, you're looking much better," the blonde says as she goes to him. She touches his face, caressing him as if he were a lover.

"Clotho, please. I beg of you, don't hurt Fiona. My faults are my own, not hers. I brought her into our world. I chased her, followed her and bedded her. She's innocent. If you must seek revenge, use me."

"But who will take care of my son, Nicolai?" Roman doesn't answer. Instead, he looks down at the ground, submitting to his creator.

"Please, not her."

"She's a human," the red-headed one says. "A servant to you, and yet you ask for her protection?"

"I do. I beg of it. Fiona does not yet know of our Covenant nor does she understand, but I will help her see our ways, to prepare her to become one of us if you so choose."

"Roman!" How dare he decide my fate without consulting with me first. If I'm to become a vampire that means... oh God, no. I would walk this earth for an eternity, never to be able to bond with him, to be with him because we would both have to choose a human consort. "No, Roman," I plead.

The raven-haired psycho beauty drags her bladed finger across my neck. My warmblood seeps down my throat. Both Roman and this other guy lick their lips, and I fear my doom is about to be met by gluttonous vampires.

"Nicolai, you should feast," the one with auburn hair says.

"NO!" Roman screams, but is held in place by the same force keeping me stable. Nicolai is in front of me in a flash and his fangs puncture my skin immediately. My eyes close, and what little life force I have in me starts to dissipate.

When Nicolai is done, he stands before me with a grin. "I want to fuck her," he says.

"And you should, my son." The blonde strokes his cheek, wiping away the remnants of my blood. I look to Roman, whose eyes are wide. He's thrashing against the confines that keep him grounded. "But you have to ask her nicely. As Roman will teach you, you can not take, what is not yours."

"But she is mine," he says. "I can feel her heart beating inside of me."

His words send a shockwave through me. The only way he can feel me, sense me, is if we are bonded. I look at Roman again, but his eyes are downcast. Our bond is no longer.

"Yeah, I'm not yours," Fiona hisses at Nicolai.

"You are too, I can feel you. And my mother says that means you're mine."

"Oh this is simply divine," Lachesis says, practically beaming.

I cannot feel the bond between Fiona and me any longer, but I still love her. I can feel that with everything I am, and I'd die to save her right now if I had to. As I watch the Sisters, they're enraptured by Nicolai and his newfound bond with my Fiona.

"Now Nicolai, you are bonded to her, but you do not have her permission so until she gives it to you, you may not fuck her. Do you understand?" Clothos coddles him.

"But why? If she's mine why can't I take her?" he whines.

"Because those are our rules!" Atropos yells at him.

"These rules are stupid. I'm hungry. And I want to fuck." Nicolai is behaving like a petulant child, and I want to strangle him.

Atropos grabs him by the neck and pulls his face to hers.

"You will obey. Or you will die. You have been given a new life full of great promise. The gift of immortality, Nicolai, which has been bestowed upon you by us, and it can be taken away by us. You will experience pain like you've never imagined if you disobey. Now shut up!" She tosses him to the ground as if he were nothing but a pebble in her hand.

This is the most fucked up scene I've encountered since I was turned. I have my creators standing before me, explaining to my new prodigy who I almost drained and killed, why he can't just fuck and eat what he wants, in reference to my human girlfriend who is now bonded to him, and not me. What the fuck is next?

Lachesis turns to her sisters. "I think we should leave things exactly as they are."

"What? You can't leave him bonded to me. I'm never going to let him lay a hand on me willingly!" Fiona yells.

"Shut up, human!" Atropos swings her finger blade at Fiona menacingly.

"Leave her alone!" I yell, still unable to move.

"All this whining! Everyone shut up, or you all die!" Atropos yells again, her voice becoming even more shrill. "Sister, what do you mean to leave things exactly as they are?"

Lachesis explains, "I cannot think of a more glorious punishment that what you see before us. Look around, Sister. They're miserable. How on earth will they find any peace or happiness? They can't. It's absolutely delightful." She laughs and points around the room as she speaks. "Roman here lost his bond to his human lover, and now his new son is bonded to her, and quite amorous as it seems. And over here, you have the human at the center of it all. In love with one, but the subject of lust for the other. They're all stuck together, with no way out. It's positively delicious."

"It would be more fun for me to kill someone." Atropos shrugs as if she's bored with what's happening around her.

"Oh, Sister," Clotho says softly. "I agree with Lachesis. I don't like it when my children die. Even if they deserve it. It makes me so sad. And I don't get to make near enough new children anymore. Let's leave them to their lives here. They stand no chance of eternal happiness. Even once the human ages and dies, Roman will still be responsible for the well being of Nicolai. I care not what happens to the human if you must kill someone, but my Nicolai likes her. Let him keep her."

"He's not keeping me. I'm not to be kept!" Fiona interjects, causing the calm and collected Clothos to hiss in her face.

"Shut. Your. Mouth, human! Before I cut your tongue out. I've had enough of you! Nicolai will remain bonded to you with or without it, so I suggest you shut up while you can still tell him no."

Fiona's face turns pale as she's told that the only thing keeping Nicolai from having his way with her at his leisure, are the rules of the Covenant, which the Sisters govern. They have given her the right to say no, and they can take it away if they wish.

"Now Nicolai, are you ready to listen and obey?" Clothos returns to her previous calm and collected demeanor.

"Yes," he replies diligently.

"That's very good, my love." She pats his head like a puppy and then turns her attention to me.

"You are to teach him the rules, as we've already told you. It is your responsibility to ensure he does not take advantage of or ruin our ability to walk the earth. He will calm with time. You may not remember everything, but you were once just like him. You wanted to eat, fuck and kill everyone in sight." She laughs and turns to Fiona, who has tears in her beautiful eyes before she continues reminding me of my responsibility. "And you did for a little while. Times were different then. But now, we must follow protocols. Agreements have been made and must be abided by. Eventually, he will find his way, but until then, you are to keep him safe. You are both my children, and I love you."

Am I supposed to say I love her back because that's not at all how I'm feeling? I want to kill her. In fact, all three of them. Not wanting to leave Fiona alone with Nicolai, I simply nod my head in agreement and understanding.

Clothos walks to Fiona and kneels in front of her. "Fiona Weston, you get to live another day it seems. I suggest you watch that mouth of yours in the future. It almost got you killed, and you haven't seen the last of me, or my Sisters, who are far less understanding than I am. We will be back to check on you. Your bond to Nicolai cannot be broken without my permission, and I do not intend to grant that permission to you in your minuscule lifetime. So, it might behoove you to give him what he desires. After all, you certainly enjoyed your time with Roman. A young, viral new vampire can give you such pleasure, Fiona. He can take you places you've only dreamed about. I suggest you consider it."

Fiona doesn't reply, and I'm so grateful for that. Her stubborn attitude could have gotten her killed today, in a way that would not have been quick and painless.

"Sisters, I think we are done here." Lachesis waves her hands around the room, which in turn frees both Fiona and me from our invisible entrapment.

"I think so too. I will be looking forward to seeing how this unexpected turn of events develops. Very well played, Sister," Atropos grins.

"Take care, my children. And Fiona, consider what I've said to you." Clothos waves, as the Sisters disappear out the sliding glass doors dramatically.

As soon as they are gone, I run to Fiona. "Are you okay?" I examine the bite marks Nicolai has left, and attempt to lick them clean for her.

"Stop!" She pushes me away.

"What?" I ask, confused.

"You're serious? Do you see what kind of fucking mess this is?"

"What do you want me to say, Fiona? A mistake was made, and now I must suffer the punishment for it. Our bond may be broken, but I love you."

Nicolai watches us, looking bored. "When can I feed on you again?"

"How about never, fucker?" Fiona snaps at him, making me laugh. She hates him, and I cannot help but be amused.

"We're bonded, you have to let me."

"You need to learn the fucking rules, pal. No means no. In human and in your crazy fucked up vampire world. So back off. We'll find you a consort later; you're not gonna starve, and the grown-ups need to sort some shit out here." Fiona schools him, and I fear I'm next.

She looks at me, narrowing her eyes. "You know what, Roman? You got me into a big pile of shit here, and it's not okay."

"I know it seems bad Fiona, but we can still have the life we want, together."

"With your college-age son on the loose, fucking everything in sight, trying to feed on me? How's this supposed to work exactly? Where do we live? Do all three of us shack up together?" Her arms are crossed, and her questions are serious. I've not considered any of them.

"I don't know, Fiona, but we can make this work. That is if you want to." I meet her eyes, searching for answers in them. "If you want us to leave you alone, I will keep him away from you, and you can lead your life as vampire free as you choose it to be."

"You're not getting off that easy, Roman."

"This is not easy for me Fiona, I promise you. Please tell me how to make this right," I beg of her.

"There is no making this right. But there is moving forward. And that's what we're going to do. I love you, Roman. That hasn't changed. Fuck them. One thing is for damn sure. I'm going to decide how things go now."

32

FIONA

*W*hen I first met Roman, I wanted nothing to do with him. Sure, he's hot, sexy, has that come fuck me smoldering look down pat, coupled with the bad boy image ... of a vampire. Did I forget to mention the added pleasure of permanent stubble that drives me absolutely wild? Sill, the fact remained, he's a walking, talking, breathing zombie without the rotten corpse. And yet, I love him, despite everything that's happened.

Today, we're cutting the ribbon on Roman's new casino. Well, actually, it's mine, but to keep the civility in our relationship, I let Roman pretend it's all his. Besides, his business sense far surpasses mine, which I suppose is a testament to his five hundred and thirty-three years of traipsing around the world, watching countries flourish, going through a depression, rising from the ashes and battling numerous wars.

To celebrate Roman's birthday, I took him to the traveling history museum where we stayed for hours, thanks to Selene, who offered to babysit Nic for us. Roman covered each era in great detail, telling me stories about the people he's met, what he did and how he served multiple countries as a soldier. I never knew my vampire was so well rounded. Mostly, I thought he sat around drinking blood and staring at the wall. It was refreshing to learn he played such an instrumental part in defining the world. I could listen to him every day, talk about the things he's experienced, how the world has changed and how some of the transformations aren't for the best.

After what Roman refers to as a "little" misunderstanding, I took a step back from our relationship, which is very hard to do when Roman and I are in love, and Nicolai and I are bonded. It's awkward, hard to explain and I've been tempted many times to change my relationship status on Facebook to "It's complicated." When I'm out and about, I'm often flanked by two vampires. The stares I receive are uncomfortable, and my relationship with Leslie no longer exists. One vampire was hard enough for her to take, throw in Nic who has no filter and no sense of personal space and Leslie bailed. Can't say I blame her. Lana, on the other hand, likes Nicolai and he loves me.

Roman and Nicolai fight, constantly. Daily, in fact. Nicolai wants to feed on me, and I refuse. I don't care if I'm breaking some Covenant or not. The law I follow says I don't have to do it, and I won't. Mostly out of vindictiveness. Although, I'm not sure who I'm spiting because to see Nicolai in pain does hurt my feelings. It's not his fault, my-couldn't-check-his-temper vampire went off the rails and tried to kill him. All of this could've been avoided if Roman wasn't so damn stubborn and refusing to accept my help. I remind him of this all the time.

Nic also wants other... things, which as his bonded mate, I suppose he has a right to request, but no. I'm not, nor will I ever be, intimate with him. This is where I don't feel sorry for him and start to resent Roman. Again, avoidable, yet I had to ask Roman to install doubled plated steel doors, which I had blessed by the same priest my father used, at my apartment to keep Roman's "son" away. I don't trust Nicolai, at least not yet. He still has some growing up to do.

Who knew a newbie vamp would be so adolescent? One too many times, I've yelled the words, "you're grounded" because of some idiotic thing Nic has done. We're talking really childish act, like walking in the garden display at the Bellagio, climbing to the top of the Luxor and jumping off the Stratosphere. I get that ordinary people don't do these sort of things, and this is probably some vampire thrill seeking activity to test his immortality, but enough is enough. Nicolai doesn't listen to Roman, only me, which means when he's doing something he's not supposed to, I get a call to come pick him up. Talk about getting the raw end of the deal, which again, I blame Roman for.

He's tried to make it up to me with offers of trips around the world (we couldn't because Nic attempted to join the mile high club as soon as we stepped onto the plane). Roman bought me the most exquisite jewels, designer clothes before they hit the rack, and offered a brand new house. I almost took him up on the home. That was until he said he and Nic would live there as well.

One big happy family.

No.

My father stands to my right and Roman to my left, both of them holding the red ribbon in place so I can make the cut. There are news crews here as well as reporters from various newspapers. My project... I mean Roman's, has become a human-interest story, bringing a multitude of human service agencies to his door. At my suggestion, Roman opened an office, hired a vampire secretary (at my urging) and started another company helping the people of Nevada with finding temporary housing, jobs and helping with some expenses, such as clothing and transportation, so people can get back on their feet.

When my father found out my deceit, he was livid and told me I was no longer a part of his family. I called his bluff and anonymously contacted the news about the project and how the Gaming Commissioner was refusing to grant the license. My dad knew I had done it and called a meeting where I laid it all out for him. He would give Roman and me, because yes, I wasn't going to give up on the project, the license needed to open the casino, and he would accept Roman as my boyfriend. The latter he balked at, threw his hands up in the air, and said over his dead body, which Nicolai took as an open invitation to kill him.

I can admit, I let Nicolai stalk my father for about thirty seconds before I told him to stop. In hindsight, I know it wasn't nice, but my father really needed to be taken down a notch. When he finally calmed down, I handed him the file I had compiled over the years. Details of his shady transactions, from as far back to when I was a teenager, placed in date order for his perusal. My demand was simple; accept Roman and subsequently Nicolai, as part of my life. That was it, nothing more.

The enormously large scissors are hard to squeeze, but I do it, slicing through the ribbon that has served as a makeshift barrier from the main door of the casino. The reporters descend on Roman and me, firing questions at us from all angles. "It's easy math," Roman tells the crowd. "We own the building outright, and after expenses are paid, the revenue will be used to continue funding the Roman Weston Home for Indigent Humans." I smile at the name of our company. It was actually Roman's idea to add my last name. I think he did it because he knows it gets on my father's nerves, but considering the Sisters strip humans of their identities and give them new names, except Nicolai, which makes me shudder just to think about, Roman never had a last name and doesn't remember his human one.

Nicolai is standing against the wall, waiting to join us. As soon as I start toward the casino, he takes his regular position on my right side. I feel sorry for him, I do, and wish there were something I do could to break our bond so he could be free. I've gone as far as to seek out a high witch priestess, hoping she can break the spell, curse or whatever it is tying him and me together.

"You look very beautiful today, Fiona."

"Thank you, Nicolai, that was a very nice compliment."

"I'd like to fuck you now."

I roll my eyes. "See, now you've gone and ruined the moment. Think before you speak." Selene and Roman believe that when he demanded to have Nicolai come feed him, Nic was actually in the middle of having sex with another vampire, hence the constant desire to have sex. Selene also believes the last conscious memory Nicolai has, is of sex and the word "fuck" which comes out of his mouth far more than it should and at the most inopportune times, like when we're standing in line at the grocery store, and he blurts it out. However, that's all he does. While I have a healthy fear of him because he's still learning the ways, he's yet to try anything but force himself on me.

Roman slaps Nicolai on his head and tells him to watch his mouth. Nic takes this to heart and strains his eyes down to his pushed out lips. "I swear the Sisters did something to his brain when they performed the ritual," Roman says. He's exhausted, and if he slept, he'd probably have sleepless nights, but as it is, he spends most of his time watching Nicolai, teaching him and trying to keep him out of trouble.

"We'll figure out how to break the bond," I tell Roman, leaning into him for a kiss. "The priestess is working to uncover ancient rituals."

"There's no guarantee," he says

I shake my head. "No, there isn't. However, until we know for sure, there isn't anything we can do about the situation." I take Roman's hand, and we walk further into the casino. Almost every table has someone sitting at it, and the slot machines are full. When Roman redesigned the layout, he put less equipment in, saying it would create more demand. So far, he looks to be right, but I have concerns.

"If people are waiting for a spot at the blackjack table, what's keeping them here as opposed to going down the street to the next casino?"

Roman smiles. There's a wicked glint in his eye. He doesn't need to answer because I already know. All the dealers at the tables are vampires, and I have a feeling, each person's being compelled to stay here.

"Roman, this is illegal."

He pulls me into his arms. "It's only illegal to compel a human into doing something they don't want to. Each one here wants to spend money. We're just enticing them to stay a little longer. Don't worry, my love, they're still in control and can say no." He winks. "Trust me, darling. You know I would never break another rule of the Covenant." This is true.

"What do you say, should we go check out the view from the Presidential suite?"

"I have a better idea."

"What's that?" I ask, only to watch Roman drop to one

knee. Already in his hand is an opened black box with a dazzling diamond sparkling under the casino lights.

"Roman!" My hand covers my mouth, and I start to nod before he even asks me anything.

"Fiona, will you give me a chance to be your husband for the rest of your life?"

"Yes, yes I will."

Roman stands and carefully places my engagement ring on my finger. Out of nowhere, Selene, Corban, Damen, Lydia, Lana and even Nicolai surround us, congratulating us. Nicolai looks hurt, which I can understand. I pull him into my arms and whisper, "Don't worry, we'll figure everything out, and you'll be free."

"And we can fuck?" he asks with a smile.

I throw my hands up in the air and start laughing, along with everyone else. This is what my life has become, surrounded by vampires as my friends, with one who has a one-track mind. If someone had asked me seven or eight months ago, what I'd be doing now, my answer would've been easy, laying by the pool, spending Daddy's money. Ask me now, and I'll tell you, running a business that helps people in need, while trying to break a bond so a man can be free to fall in love, and not upset three Sisters who are hell-bent on making sure I pay for my vampire's mistake.

Nicolai

Coming in August

ACKNOWLEDGMENTS

Heidi and Amy want to thank you for taking a chance on our vampire. We sincerely hope you enjoyed our little tale and will stick around for Nicolai's book, which will come out in August.

Huge shout-out to our team: Kellie Montgomery, Letitia Hasser and Ena & Amanda from Enticing Book Journey. As well as everyone on our street teams for making sure our teasers were shared, our story made sense, and for telling us how hot Roman is!

Also, we want to thank Bram Stroker for giving us something to sink our teeth into!

ABOUT HEIDI MCLAUGHLIN

Heidi McLaughlin is a New York Times, Wall Street Journal, and USA Today Bestselling author of The Beaumont Series, The Boys of Summer, and The Archers.

Originally, from the Pacific Northwest, she now lives in picturesque Vermont, with her husband, two daughters, and their three dogs.

In 2012, Heidi turned her passion for reading into a full-fledged literary career, writing over twenty novels, including the acclaimed Forever My Girl.

When writing isn't occupying her time, you can find her sitting courtside at either of her daughters' basketball games.

Heidi's first novel, Forever My Girl, has been adapted into a motion picture with LD Entertainment and Roadside Attractions, starring Alex Roe and Jessica Rothe, and opened in theaters on January 19, 2018.

Don't miss more books by Heidi McLaughlin! Sign up for her newsletter, or join the fun in her fan group!

Connect with Heidi!
www.heidimclaughlin.com

ABOUT AMY BRIGGS

Amy Briggs is a Texas based writer. Formerly a firefighter and EMT in New Jersey living next to a military base, Amy was initially drawn to creating stories around emergency services and the military, and draws on her experiences to show the depth and emotional side of the lifestyle. Her love of fairy tales carries through each of her novels and she hopes to inspire readers to fall in love with love.

Have all things Amy Briggs delivered to your email? Join her mailing list!
Don't forget to follow Amy on Instagram!

You can also reach Amy at the following:
amybriggs.author@gmail.com

ALSO BY HEIDI MCLAUGHLIN

THE BEAUMONT SERIES

Forever My Girl – Beaumont Series #1

My Everything – Beaumont Series #1.5

My Unexpected Forever – Beaumont Series #2

Finding My Forever – Beaumont Series #3

Finding My Way – Beaumont Series #4

12 Days of Forever – Beaumont Series #4.5

My Kind of Forever – Beaumont Series #5

Forever Our Boys - Beaumont Series #5.5

The Beaumont Boxed Set - #1

THE BEAUMONT SERIES: NEXT GENERATION

Holding Onto Forever

My Unexpected Love

THE ARCHER BROTHERS

Here with Me

Choose Me

Save Me

LOST IN YOU SERIES

Lost in You

Lost in Us

THE BOYS OF SUMMER

Third Base

Home Run

Grand Slam

THE REALITY DUET

Blind Reality

Twisted Reality

SOCIETY X

Dark Room

Viewing Room

Play Room

STANDALONE NOVELS

Stripped Bare

Blow

Sexcation

Santa's Secret

ALSO BY AMY BRIGGS

SNEAK PEEK OF MY UNEXPECTED LOVE

BY HEIDI MCLAUGHLIN

Elle

My head rests against the glass of the backseat window. Raindrops slide down, one meeting the other, forming a longer stream of water. Each one's only visible when we happen to pass under a streetlight. The edge of my finger-nail follows the path until the small ball of water at the end meets the bottom of the window. I glance quickly at my phone, pressing the home button to bring it to life, only the solid black screen stares back at me.

It's dead, like how I feel on the inside.

"What time is it?" My voice is garbled and my breath poisoned by the harsh aftertaste of vodka, tequila, and what-ever else I managed to get my hands on, causing my stomach to twist. Being underage hasn't stopped me from hitting every hotspot in Los Angeles, nor has it stopped the bouncers from letting me in. They all know who I am and not a single one of them cares because they know I'm there to spend money. Not to mention, I bring an entourage with me. For the club, it's free promotion considering every one of my friends details our outings on social media.

"Just after three." The driver's foreign accent makes it sound like he said tree or maybe it was free. My mind is mush, and I feel like I'm on the verge of passing out. I lift my head to glance at his GPS, only to have a wave of nausea roll through me. I press my forehead back to the cold window and close my eyes.

"How much longer?"

"We're here." The car comes to an abrupt stop, throwing my body forward. I look into the rearview mirror and meet the driver's eyes, and I swear he smirks. Blindly, I ruffle through my bag and pull out a twenty. The rate on the dash reads nineteen and some change.

"Here ya go." I toss the bill at him and exit the car. He screeches away within seconds of me closing the door. "Asshole," I mutter into the darkness.

Each step I take toward the apartment I share with my brother Quinn is painful. Tonight's outing is definitely one for the record books. Aside from the copious amounts of flowing alcohol, the all-night dancing has done a number on my muscles.

I don't know how long it takes with me fumbling around, trying to get my key in the lock before it opens. Quinn stands there, with his arm holding the door. The muscles in his arm strains, likely from the grip he has on the edge of the wood. The bright light from our living room lamp highlights his scowl almost perfectly, which is different for him because usually, Quinn's expressionless, always stoic. It's the troubled soul of a musician, only he's not troubled. I swear if he were, I don't think I'd be able to live with him.

"Thanks." I step in, brushing against him.

"We need to talk, Elle."

"Did someone die?" This is my automatic response to a statement like this. Quinn looks at me, his eyes cold and steady. I shrug. I know it's a bad joke, but whatever. I don't know why he expects anything different from me.

The door slams shut. The sound reverberates through the room, causing me to jump. "All right, can we at least turn the light off?" I shield my eyes when I look at him, exaggerating the fact that the light is too bright. His expression seems to worsen as he glares at me.

"Sit down." Quinn's command is forceful, demanding. He points to one of the two chairs we own. He's set them up across from one another in the middle of our living room, almost like an interrogation or better yet an intervention.

"What's going on?" I sit with a huff, slouching in the chair with my legs kicked out in front of me. My brother sits down and grips the armrests, keeping his back straight and his eyes set on mine. Quinn is hard to read, always has been. I'm not joking when I say he's a tortured or troubled musician, even though he grew up in the lap of luxury. The stigma still applies to him. He's an old soul, according to our grandma, and carries some imaginary burden that only Quinn knows how to combat. "Quinn?"

"The partying has to stop, Elle."

"Excuse me?"

"I didn't stutter. Since... for the past year, you've been out of control. Most nights, you don't even make it home. At first, I didn't think it was anything. Nothing out of the ordinary, since you're in college and this is what kids our age do, but recently, your habits are all over social media and Mom and Dad are throwing around words like court-ordered rehab."

My mouth suddenly dries, my stomach rolls and my

temper is on the verge of exploding. No one, not Quinn, my parents or even my sister can understand what I've been going through. What Quinn couldn't bring himself to say is that since my twin sister almost died, since she was smashed up in a car, much like our father, and had to fight for her life, I haven't been right. Nothing in my life seems right anymore, and partying is the only way I know how to cope. The drinking allows me to stay numb, it keeps my mind in a fog, so I don't have to deal with the endless questions about how I'm doing, how Peyton is coming along or when am I going to settle down like her. The constant comparison, whether it's about our physical health or mental well-being is taking its toll. People seem to forget that we're twins, but we're not the same person. "You have no right."

"I have every right. I'm tired of watching you self-destruct. I was there too, Elle. I almost lost my sister as well, but you don't see me drowning myself night after night, with people who don't care about me, who won't protect me if something were to go wrong."

"No, you're perfect, right? You don't let anything affect you. You don't drink, do drugs or attempt to live life! You sit in your room, and write your songs, day after day and play them night after night at whatever bar or coffee shop will let you, until you get your big break. You sing to people who don't care about you, who won't rescue you if something were to go wrong. Seems we're not much different in the way we're coping."

Quinn shakes his head. "I'm not coping, Elle. I've moved on. I've come to terms with the fact Peyton almost died. It took me months, but you, it's... this has to stop. No one's saying you can't go out and have fun, but night after night drunken escapades have to come to an end. We are all in agreement, things have to change."

"Who's we?"

"Mom and Dad. Peyton and I. Ben."

"Ben?" My eyes divert to Quinn's, and he nods. I shake my head, wondering when my best friend decided to betray me. He's supposed to be my ride or die, but lately, he's been distant, standoffish. Maybe this is why. Could it be he's had enough of my crap and is trying to put some space between us? No, I don't believe it. If anything, he's got his nose to the books and is preparing for our upcoming finals.

"He's worried about you. We all are."

"None of you knows anything about me." My hands push into my hair as I grunt. I want to scream, to shove Quinn against the wall and yell until he finally understands what it's like to be me, if only for five minutes. Be Elle Powell-James, sister of Peyton who is engaged to Noah Westbury, and living their happy little life on social media for everyone to see. I shouldn't think this way when it comes to my sister because she's my lifeline, my best friend. There isn't anything I wouldn't do for her, and if she knew how I felt, she'd crumble. The last thing she would ever want to do is hurt me.

Quinn sighs and rubs his hands down the front of his legs. He's dressed like our dad, khaki shorts with combat boots with some random band shirt, likely a group from the seventies when 'music was real' and made with instruments and not computers.

"Dad received a call earlier tonight. He called me looking for you because your cell was going to voicemail."

"It's dead."

Quinn nods. "Anyway, I'm sure you know how your night went, but Mom and Dad received an eyeful when some journalists sent them pictures of you. I had to talk Dad into staying home, but he's angry, Elle."

"Well, his sister didn't almost die, did she?"

"At some point, Peyton's accident can no longer be your excuse. You used it to ditch out of a semester of school. You've used it for your grades and now this."

I turn away when I feel unshed tears threatening to escape. My throat tightens, and my body starts to ache. The impending onslaught of tears makes it hard to speak.

"These people you're hanging out with are making sure everyone knows everything about you. Every night they post videos of the person we love, falling down drunk, hanging on strange men, and almost passed out in random clubs, for our viewing pleasure."

"I haven't seen anything like that. How do I know you're not making this up?"

"Why would I? Why would I stay up until after three a.m. to have this talk with you if I were making any of this up? I value my sleep, Elle."

"My friends wouldn't do this."

"They're not your friends. They're leeches, using you for your connections. They're using you for the star power that comes with saying they've hung out with you. They don't care about you, no more than you care about them. How do you think Mom feels when she sees her daughter like that? Or Dad? Or the industry? You want to be a manager, but who's going to bring you on staff when they can Google you and see what your lifestyle is like. Like it or not, we're expected to act a certain way, behave as respected adults in the community. I don't think our parents are asking too much of us."

"And what if I don't want to, huh?" My tone is defiant and harsh.

"You don't have a choice."

"Says who?"

Quinn adjusts in the chair. He pulls out his phone, and by his movements, I'm guessing he's thumbing through his apps. He clears his throat. "Mr. and Mrs. James, We're writing to let you know our facility can accommodate Elle Powell-James when you see fit to admit her. Please note, this is an intense ninety-day treatment and visitors will not be allowed unless family counseling is needed. We will restrict all outside communications as well. We have a strict paparazzi rule, and our guards will ensure that all photographers are kept off the property to protect Elle's privacy. Once you have your legal affairs in order, please let us know."

I swallow hard as I try to understand what Quinn is reading, and am unable to hold my tears at bay any longer. My parents aren't messing around, but what they don't understand is, I'm an adult, and I can make my own decisions. If I want to party, I can. If I want to drop out of school, I can. If I want...

"As you can see, Mom and Dad have had enough." Quinn interrupts my thoughts. "And I think you know this, which is why you've been ignoring their calls, not going home to see them and dodging their visits."

"I haven't--"

"You have. Before Peyton's accident, you and Mom spoke daily. When's the last time you spoke with her? When's the last time you've been home? If I had to guess it was when Peyton was living there, but you haven't been back since."

"Texting is easier."

"Only because you can avoid the elephant in the room. You need help, Elle."

"I'm not going to some celebrity rehab center, Quinn."

"Then stop!" His voice echoes off the walls. "Grow up

and start acting like someone who has a future instead of the Hollywood cliché."

"I'm not--"

"You are. That's what gets me the most, Elle. This person you've become is the same person you've mocked since you moved here. All our lives, you've said you'd never become the socialite who uses her name to get into clubs or restaurants, and now look at you. You've become the epitome of someone you despise."

"You don't understand."

Quinn nods. "I know, Elle. Peyton almost died. You're twins, you felt it. I've heard every excuse you can come up with, blaming whatever it is you have going on, on Peyton and the accident." He adjusts in the chair and leans forward with his arms resting on his legs. "Peyton's healed. She's moved on. She's planning a wedding, finishing college and trying to make peace with her life. If she can do that, then so can you." He taps my leg before getting up and leaving the room. I glance at the empty space Quinn's left behind. The bright light blinds me, causing me to turn away. As soon as I hear Quinn's door shut, I let the tears flow and the anger build. No one is going to tell me what to do with my life.

For More Information visit
Heidi's Website

SNEAK PEEK OF FIRED UP

BY AMY BRIGGS

Josie

I can't find anything appropriate to wear to my own dad's funeral. Everyone is going to be there, wearing their Class A Uniforms, which is totally appropriate, he was a Fire District Chief, but I'm not wearing mine. I haven't worked at his department in over a year, and it just doesn't seem appropriate at all. My aunt also said that my father's only daughter shouldn't be dressed like a boy the day he's laid to rest, so there's that too.

At least my best friend Matt will be there, and I also know his brother Brian is going to be there, he was actually appointed into my father's position when he died last week. Brian and I have a history. We had a moment really; a hot, steamy moment that I'll never be able to get out of my head apparently. I felt a moistness between my legs thinking about his beautiful green eyes, his well defined muscles and the tattoos that couldn't be more perfectly placed on his chest and arms..., *Jesus Christ its your dad's funeral, get your shit together Josephine Meadows*. That was a one time thing, it was just kiss, a really great kiss, and this is neither the time nor place for these thoughts. And Brian was a cocky asshole anyway.

Matt was picking my aunt and I up, she was my only family left now and my dad's older sister. My mom died when I was three, leaving me and my dad to fend for ourselves. He never dated, or married again; he was more or less married to the fire service anyway. That's how he ended up dying, on a fire call, of a heart attack. It was no secret that the stress of firefighting made heart attacks the number one killer of firefighters, but their shitty diets certainly didn't help either.

"Josephine!!! Matt is here, let's go!" Aunt Molly yelled from downstairs. I finished putting on my favorite red lipstick, grabbed some black heels that were probably a bit too high for walking around all day and took a deep breathe as I went downstairs. This was going to be a long day, but these were all of the people that cared about my dad, really, they were our family.